Before t

Slipper

The *Before* Series

Book 1

Michelle Deerwester-
Dalrymple

Author's Note:

This book is not a traditional romance. Instead of steamy romance, these reads are a bit darker and follows the sad lives of our favorite villains before their infamous stories. Please be ready for something a bit darker, not steamy, and perhaps not the happy, fairy-tale ending we are used to!

If you love this book, be sure to leave a review! Reviews are life blood for authors, and I appreciate every review I receive!

Love what you read? Want more from Michelle? Go online to the website listed below to receive *The Heartbreak of the Glen*, the free Glen Highland Romance short ebook, free books, updates, and more in your inbox.

https://linktr.ee/mddalrympleauthor

Table of Contents

Chapter One

"MOTHER, PLEASE. DON'T make me do this," I begged.

Over and over, I had begged, pleaded, even tried bribing, but to no avail. I was going to have to wed the miserable Seigneur Dubois in a fortnight, and no recourse had made itself known. From the tight lines around my mother's eyes, she was tired of hearing my protests.

"Corinne, I'll not have you behaving like this. I'm finished with this conversation, and so is your father. You will marry Seigneur Andre Dubois and be grateful. So many girls your age would be ecstatic to wed as accomplished a man as Andre."

Accomplished. That was a code word for old. And wealthy. Those were the sole concerns my parents had for my future. Marrying for love? They'd scoffed at the idea and sent me to my room. Then they had accepted the old man's offer on my behalf.

I understood their concerns. Father had worked hard as a merchant, buying rugs, furs, and fabrics from the docks and selling them to upscale lords, *comptes*, and even a few dukes, but local wars and pirating had plagued the shores of La Rochelle to the bustling town of Poitiers, and fewer goods had become available. Father's financial well-being had started to fall down the path to ruin. Plus, to hear Father tell it, the King's taxes had made his finances worse. They needed a solution, something to keep them in their home for the rest of their lives.

So they were *selling* me. No matter what pretty packaging they tried to wrap the news in, that was the ugly truth.

"Mother," I tried once more. Mother angrily waggled a finger at me.

"I'm finished. Now, go to your chambers and have Elise finish helping you pack. The seamstress will be here this afternoon to complete your gown. And your bridegroom is generous and sent you a fine wedding gift. I'll show you when you try on your dress." Here, her face brightened, the first time I'd seen such a look in longer than I cared to think on. "It is the most refined gift. You'll love it."

She may have been trying to sweeten the pot, but I knew it was nothing more than additional bows on the horrible present I was set to unwrap. I shuddered; the idea of unwrapping anything with regards to my bridegroom made my gorge rise.

When I entered my room, Elise gave me a gentle, closed-mouth smile. She was the only one in the house who commiserated with my plight. A plain, silver-edged glass hung near my water table, and I looked away. Since the announcement of my impending nuptials, I had avoided seeing reflections of myself anywhere, because it was my dark, ethereal beauty that put me into this position to begin with.

Andre was a customer of my father's, but instead of purchasing a small plot of land and house,

Andre Dubois had inherited his, a much larger plot, and was considered a significant lord in our remote, hilly country. But even fine lords had problems with rats, I'd learned, and when the rug in his salon was shredded by the vermin, Seigneur Dubois had taken two steps to fix his situation. He'd adopted a series of cats for the house and the barn, and he'd visited Monsieur Minuet.

Andre had arrived unannounced to the humble Minuet home. The narrow two-story house had dwarfed when the portly Andre entered the main room, his girth filling it, just as much as his unpleasant odor. I didn't know if that was his odor or if it was a result of his age, but the scent had lingered in the room long after he departed, and Mother had brought in wild roses from the yard so their heady scents might drive out his onerous, moldy smell.

Father had met the man in the main room, and shouted over his shoulder that Mother and I should bring refreshments while he arranged the rugs he had for the fine lord to peruse. He was a nice enough man, with a kind smile for Mother and me as he selected a watercress sandwich from Mother's platter.

That was when Seigneur Dubois took another decisive step. Before he left, he asked my father for my hand. And promised a significant payment in return.

I don't know what the man saw in me. Who asks for a woman's hand in marriage after a single, brief meeting?

Other girls in the village were prettier than I, at least in my estimation. My most notable feature had to be my long neck — as elegant as a swan's, my mother often claimed — that dropped to my clear milky chest. Otherwise, I wore my black hair simply, a few locks pulled back and held in place with pins that day. My height, oft viewed by my parents as a detriment to any hopes of finding a husband, meant my clothes hung on my frame if they weren't properly fitted. When I did wear my more fitted gown, my mother vowed no more beautiful lass existed in the land. So evidently, my height wasn't as great a problem as my parents believed.

On the day Andre met me, my aprons cinched my waist and my ebony hair fell across my chest, where I am sure drew my unadorned décolletage to his attention. My deft hands poured his tea with ease, and his eyes never left me as he took the chipped saucer from my fingers. I could see it in his face, his watery eyes that roved over me as if he already owned me, and for men of power, perchance that was true.

His power, his money — often men, and women, believed wealth could solve any ill.

I wanted love. I craved it. I wanted to marry my soul mate — not be sold off at the ripe age of seventeen to a cranky old man. Like I was cattle. And while it was possible for men of his stature to find love, I didn't think it was my love he was going to find. My heart was set on more youthful, girlhood dreams.

"Milady, can ye make some decisions about your trunk? Do ye want to pack your work kirtles in addition to your gown? I dinna think ye will need them . . ."

Elise patted the fine gown atop the rest. A gold and green brocade with a thin filigree pattern, 'twas the finest gown I owned. My pale blue surely was tucked right beneath that, with my one linen chemise. My work dress hung from a peg on the back of my door. My only other gown, the deep brown I presently wore, hid stains well. I decided to wear this to meet my future husband. I didn't care.

My eyes flicked to the pallid sunlight pouring through the window. After a day of rain, the sunshine, peeking from behind the clouds as best it could, was a welcome reprieve. The lone bright spot in this otherwise dismal day.

I'm not sure what Elise thought I was considering, but she clicked her tongue at me as she folded up my one set of clean stockings and placed them atop the gowns in the trunk.

"Dinna think of climbing or jumping, milady," Elise spoke without looking at me. "The distance is too far and ye will break your leg, for certain, if ye jump. And if ye try to climb down the ivy, even if it supported your weight, your father would send the sheriff after ye in a thrice. Ye'd no' get far enough."

I fairly blanched at Elise's proposition. I hadn't considered running away! Elise possessed a darker side than she showed, and the corner of my mouth pulled up into a slight smile for the first time in days.

"Elise! Such a reckless *fille* you are! I had no idea you might strategize so nefarious an escape plan!"

She shrugged, but the lines of her face softened. "I just worry for ye, Lady Corinne."

I sat on my sagging bed and watched her pack for me.

She wasn't the only one who worried.

I laid on my bed, studying the shadows dancing across the wood-beamed ceiling when the seamstress burst through the door. Elise had departed an hour ago, closing my door with another clicking of her tongue. I shot up in the center of the bed at the surprise interruption of my dire thoughts.

The seamstress, a short, portly woman with lines around her eyes and mouth, talent in her hands, and the unfortunate name of Morga. She smiled widely at my disheveled state.

"Corinne! Get down here, and let's see how the gown looks on you! Your mother is on her way up, and I believe you will both be pleased beyond measure."

It was difficult not to be caught up in Morga's excitement, but I bit my tongue and gave her a sour smile. I was determined to hate the dress, no matter what.

And if my words were cake, I'd have eaten them. The dress was well crafted, fit for a country gentleman's bride. I loved it the moment I laid eyes on it.

A light green with white folds and white ribbon crossed along the back to secure the bodice. White and moss green ribbon hung from the short sleeves, and the skirts fell in soft folds to my toes. I hated to admit it, hated it to my bones, but the dress was beautiful. Not a princess dress, but nicer than anything I'd ever owned. It made my brocade look like a carpet.

"You can wear your leather slippers," my mother directed as she walked around me, evaluating every stitch. With gentle fingers, she pulled my black hair over my shoulder. The contrast of the light fabric against my hair wasn't lost on me.

"And we can weave a few ribbons in your hair, matching the gown. Your groom will be beside himself," Morga added.

The reminder of the dour man I was to marry popped my bubble, and the glow of the day departed. My mother noticed.

"That is fine, Morga. Let us get the dress off her and hang it until the big day. If you join me downstairs, I will make sure Monsieur Minuet pays you."

My mother's lips tightened as she spoke the words, at the prospect of parting with coin. That woman could grip onto silver tighter than anyone. The seamstress unlaced my bodice and shook her head as I slithered out of the fine gown.

"Nay, milady. Seigneur Dubois has already paid me for my services. A wedding gift for his bride."

My mother nodded, relief soothing her clenched features.

At least something about this day pleased her. My heart, in a rare move, thrummed in my chest for her. Just how bad were my father's finances?

Once everyone left and the sun began to set, I cleaned up from our evening meal and retreated to my room, one of my last times that I would be able to do so. I'd changed from my brown wool into a clean shift after washing my hands, face, and neck. A cool spring breeze blew through the open window, carrying the scents of hyacinth and lilies on its back.

Elise's bold words returned to me. I went to my window and leaned farther out, bending fretfully at the waist. She'd been right, of course. Too far to jump without injury, and the weak tendrils of ivy wouldn't support anything other than leaves or tiny birds. No out for me there.

Not that any out existed. In a few days, I would become Madame Corinne Dubois, and nothing was going to stop it. I shuddered again, not from the cool breeze, and pulled myself back into the room. The window received the brunt of my simmering anger, and I slammed down the sash, cracking the painted wood.

Chapter Two

I TRIED TO RECALL the beauty of my wedding day to Andre Dubois, and forget the miserable parts, including my wedding night. I stuffed every single one of those horrible memories into a box inside my head and packed them away – far away into the darkest shadows of my being. I did my best to focus on the moments of joy I did experience that day.

Family and friends from the countryside surrounding Poitiers joined us for my nuptials at the country church. The sun shone brightly again, teasing me by having stunning light on so dark a day for me. But the light did catch on the few stained-glass windows high in the church, casting the interior into a cacophony of colors. That I remembered.

We spoke our vows fast, too fast, and I needed to catch my breath. I couldn't breathe at all. My eyes latched on to the priest, begging him to see me, see my gray eyes and blanched skin and call the wedding off.

The man scarcely glanced at me. He declared Andre and I man and wife, and then Andre was kissing me, his breath reeking of stale fish. I held my breath and bit back a cough as his rough lips slapped against mine. We are of a similar height, so the kiss was easy to catch, and just as easy for me to push away.

It was done. I was married.

Seigneur Dubois and his household put out a fine spread of food for a post-wedding feast, but I ate nothing. My stomach was in knots, twisting and turning as my new husband sat next to me in his rich velvet finery, sweating as he ate through the remnants of a game hen. A dollop of cherry conserve streaked across the plate every time he dipped his meat into the red sauce.

I hated cherry conserve. Was he going to kiss me with that cherry-stained mouth? My gorge rose, and I had to choke it back.

"Are you not hungry, wife?" Dubois asked as he patted my knee. I tried not to react. He had to know I didn't want to marry him; it would do no good for him to see that I reviled him.

Several rounds of cheers rose among my family and Dubois's friends, who gathered in his main hall.

Chateau Dubois wasn't a palace by any means, but it put my humble home to shame. Our entire downstairs could fit into his gathering hall. I flicked my eyes to the curved stairs that led to an expansive upper level where I assumed the master's chambers would be. My chambers that I'd share with this decrepit man. I tried to suppress it, but my shudder overwhelmed me. I lifted my cut crystal glass and plastered a fake smile on my face.

Then I drank. A lot. There wasn't enough of the golden liquid in Pointier for me that day.

Too soon, my mother took my hand and walked me up the stairs. At the last minute, my spinning head remembered to lift my skirts as I walked, lest I tumbled down on my backside. I glanced at the bottom of the stairs, considering that I might avoid this night if I did take a fall. Then my mother tugged on my hand, and I continued my march to the inevitable ending of what should have been my happiest day.

"You know what to do, *oui, ma chou*?" my mother asked me as she stripped off the beautiful gown and hung it in the etched wardrobe.

I looked away, trying to find a point of interest in my embroidered kirtle.

"*Oui,* Maman. I know what to do. You explained my task well."

"Well, then," she stood and patted her skirts. She bent quickly and kissed my cool cheek. "This is a good thing for you, Corinne. Please remember that. Make your husband happy and you will find joy all the days of your life."

She spun away, leaving me to stand in the middle of a dim room that wasn't mine, preparing to sleep in a bed that wasn't mine, to give to my groom my body that was no longer mine.

"Easy for you to say," I said to no one and sat on the bed to wait for my husband.

It was good the wine flowed like water on my wedding day, because my husband was too drunk to do much more than get his husbandly duty done. At least, that was how it seemed compared to what my mother described. Then he fell asleep and snored for the rest of the night.

And that was most of my first year of married life. I didn't know if his behavior was due to his age or his over-consumption of cheese, meat, and wine, but he didn't make many demands on me as a wife.

But from the few demands he did make upon me, he must have done something right, because a few months later I was pregnant. And as I grew full with our child, that fullness drove away most of my irritations with Andre, the baby not leaving any room for my negativity. I actually grew to care for Andre, a bit. Not love, not at all, but care, concern, yes.

I wasn't sure how Dubois would receive the news. He didn't have children, so I assumed a son would be welcome. What if I carried a girl?

During the first weeks when I came to learn of my new state, I spent them as I did most of my days, wandering around the small estate in a fine gown procured by Andre. I was fortunate, as wives went. Andre doted on me. Within the first week of our marriage, he had the seamstress visit and three new gowns made — a casual one of blue lawn with lace dangling from the sleeves, a rich green velvet, and a blue and gold brocade, not unlike the gown I brought from home.

Promenading around the house, touching the glass and bronze *objet d'arts,* the new carpets my father had procured cushioned my feet in my new leather slippers, and during the day I escaped to the barn and played with the kids and baby chicks. I rarely raised a finger in work, as the Lord Dubois had a small cadre of house help. At most, I helped my husband dress in the morning, wrapping his belly in a girdle so his shirts might fit, and then undressed him in the eve.

Truly, some days I felt like a queen.

Most days, though, sadness ran through me in a flood. I didn't love my husband. He cared for me, perchance loved me, but not in the way I wanted or expected. Not in the way depicted in art or in stories of old. That was the love I longed for, and for all its glided beauty, this house was empty. Devoid of true love. Devoid of joy.

Thus, telling my husband of this baby unnerved me. Would news of the baby bring missing joy and love to my life? Or would it further accentuate the emptiness?

Dinner was a solitary affair, the two of us sitting at the table of everyday linens, he at the head and myself to his right. While my dresses still fit well, they pulled a bit tighter at the waist. The women of the house staff would take notice soon. Better to tell Andre before they did.

I tapped my silver spoon against my blue edged porcelain bowl. The soup was bland, more watery broth than meat or vegetable. I took a deep breath.

"Andre, my husband, I have good news."

He didn't stop eating and mumbled "Mmm?" As he shoveled another spoonful of the sorry excuse for soup into his mouth.

"I am with child. We are to start our family."

I held my breath longer than I thought possible, waiting for him to respond. My gaze remained riveted on my soup bowl, and I dared to peek at him from the corner of my eye.

That news garnered Andre's attention. He wiped his face with his napkin and, turning to me, took my hand in his.

"Corinne, are you speaking the truth? You are with child?"

The awe in his voice softened my heart. He *was* a good man. I may have wanted something different in a husband, but he was noble and didn't deserve my disdain. From the sound of his voice, it was as if I gave him the greatest gift known to man.

And maybe I had.

"A child? Mayhap a son? Oh, Corinne!" He tugged his girth from his chair and somehow managed to kneel in front of me. He placed his head on my lap as his hand curved around my belly.

"What if 'tis a daughter, Andre?" I risked asking. His belly quivered against my legs.

"Then she shall be more spoiled than her mother," he promised.

In that moment, I could almost love him.

Almost.

Chapter Three

GENEVIEVE DUBOIS WAS born six months later, squealing into this world. She was perfect, with hair as black as mine standing up on end, and every finger and toe as beautifully formed as could be. She was a true gift. Andre feared holding her once the midwife deemed Genevieve hale, and he couldn't pull his gaze from her swaddled face.

Our relationship, though it began strained and uncomfortable, had grown to one of respect and even joy, brought on by the birth of our daughter. All the love I couldn't express for Andre, I showered on

Genevieve. And if Andre loved me, he adored our little girl.

"Oh, *mon amour*, you have truly gifted me with a new life. First your hand in marriage, then a child. Never had there been a happier man."

I was packed in cloth, pale and worn, and barely heard a word he said.

Andre had spoken the truth about our daughter. He pushed through his age and doted on Genevieve whenever he could. The house was full of giggles and the joy I had sought.

This blue-eyed, black-haired beauty brought me pride I never thought possible. My heart swelled in my chest whenever I looked at her tiny face, those needy fingers. Now when I roamed the house or the barn, I brought her with me.

And though I loved her, loved her with a wild frenzy unknown in this world, my heart near shattering when she called out "Maman" for the first time, it wasn't the love I had searched for.

"Oh, dear Genevieve, I promise I shall love you and put you first in my life for all my days," I promised as her tiny finger wrapped around mine.

Nothing could come between my daughter and me.

Two years later, another daughter shone the light of joy into my life, a doe-eyed, russet-brown haired lassie we name Finette. She, too, was a vision of perfection, my joy, and though Andre vowed to dote on her and spoil her as much as her sister, the disappointment in his face was evident, evident even to my worn-out eye.

He had wanted a son. It was the way of men. I promised him our third child, surely, must be a boy. Andre gave me a weak smile and handed our daughter to her nursemaid. I closed my eyes, cursing myself for the statement.

Andre was never destined to have his boy. He tried to spend time with his daughters, play with the now-rambunctious Genevieve who had a question for every minute of the day and didn't sit still for anything. His age and his health, however, had other plans. Andre struggled to keep up with Genevieve and her questions. Often, even holding Finette seemed to wear him out.

And I was worried. What would happen to my daughters and me if something happened to Andre? Had he provided for us? I didn't know where his money came from or what happened if he didn't have a son. Would we still live in his house? On his land?

When I asked him, he patted my arm and assured me we were cared for.

I never should have trusted his word. Husbands lie, I learned, to quiet their wives.

Andre died on a Tuesday. He went to bed the night before, kissed my cheek, and rolled on his side. When I slipped out of bed in the morn, he didn't stir, and when he didn't call for my help to dress, I grew worried. He didn't move when I shook him awake, and I called for the coachman to retrieve a doctor.

It was too late. I knew that before I called for the coachman. The doctor served no purpose to Andre. He'd be useful to me, though, to arrange for Andre's funeral.

Once the doctor departed with the body to deliver it to the church and offering me empty condolences, I took to Andre's study.

The room was rife with Andre — rich with dark wooden walls and trim, a heavy desk facing a long, beveled glass window, and shelves of books and knickknacks lining the far wall. A quill and ink sat on the edge of the desk near a stack of papers, highlighted by a shaft of late afternoon sunlight. Legal papers? Land papers? His manuscript? I didn't know. And that was the problem.

Rifling through his papers and books, I searched for something, anything that might detail how we were to live now that he was gone. Where were his accounts? How did he collect rents? Where was the money for the upkeep on the manse? My heart was in my throat the entire time, choking me more and more as I searched.

A wooden box filled with francs. A paper guaranteeing the land to Andre and to pass to his son. The name of his solicitor. That was all.

I grabbed the paper and stuck it into the box with the money, then gathering my skirts, took the box to our bed chambers. Now my bed chambers.

The maid had changed the linen, so I might sleep on crisp bedding, not sheets filled with death and decay. A slender table with my hair combs and silver-lined looking glass resting atop sat in the corner of the room, and there I sat, sweeping my toiletries to the side to make room for this box.

In the morning I'd have to send Mattias for the solicitor, if word hadn't gotten to the town by then. I expected the solicitor to be at my door by the time I woke.

A gentle knock at the door drew me from my thoughts. I turned to see wee Genevieve's ebony head peeking around the door. She resembled an angel sent to save me from myself, and perhaps that was the truth. I was tired, worn, my skin sallow from the weight of the day, and I needed someone to save me. My little girl was the savior I needed right then.

"Come to Maman, sweet."

She raced to me, her little feet bare and filthy, a stark contrast to the ruffle of her pinafore. She was a doll, my Genevieve.

"Maman. You are sad. Finette is sad too. Why is everyone sad? And where has papa gone?" she asked as she climbed up my skirts.

A rush of burning tears scorched my eyes, and I blinked rapidly to hide my sadness, my fears, from this angel on my lap.

"Do you recall at church, when the priests talk of heaven, and how wonderful it will be to go there?" I didn't know what to say to her. How does one describe death to a child who had the fullness of life still ahead of them?

She nodded and stuck a finger in her mouth before resting her head on my bosom. The warm weight of her body on mine was the solace I craved to calm my soul.

"*Oui*, Maman," she said around her finger.

"Your father had left this mortal coil and has gone to heaven."

"Oh! But I will miss him! When can I visit him?" Her little voice shattered my heart.

"Not for a long time, my little Ginny. But we shall be the best little girl we can, so he will be proud of us when we do meet him again, won't we?"

Genevieve nodded, tucking herself into my bosom even more. Her bedtime loomed, but this night I didn't press. I needed her tucked into me as much as she needed it. And when she began to doze, I put her in my bed. I might not have a husband in my bed, but I wasn't going to sleep alone.

And I didn't for a long time. Soon Finette joined us as well, and for the next two years, we all slept in that large bed together.

Chapter Four

I SAT AT ANDRE'S desk for another night, counting the money left in the box. So little left. How had I gone through so much? More importantly, how was I to get more money?

Shortly after the burial, Andre's solicitor had told me that as long as I could pay for the upkeep on the house and the land, I could stay. But technically, the resources from the property were delegated to Andre's nephew. He traveled, didn't need the house, so my daughters and I had a roof over our heads.

But no money to pay for it. What sense did it make for his nephew to make the income and not have to pay for any of the house upkeep? A heavy bitterness enveloped my heart, choking it every time I thought about Andre's greedy nephew. He hadn't sent a franc to us in assistance. How could he be so despicable to his own family?

I tapped my fingertip against the box, trying to gather my thoughts. There had to be a way to make money. I couldn't work as a governess — my daughters needed me, and I lived in my home. I couldn't very well live with another family and raise their children.

My father's textiles were doing well, but he didn't have a position for a woman with children in his business. What did that leave? Selling fruit in the market? I flicked my eyes to the darkened window. Our garden grew scant enough food for the girls and myself, and the shell of a house staff I still employed. If things kept up as they did, I might have to let another girl go.

The tightness in my chest clenched all the more at that thought. Did the nephew not understand that not only my livelihood, but the care of an entire household was at stake?

No, he must not. No single man could be so cruel as to let us suffer so.

"Maman. Are we going to bed soon?" a tiny voice called from the doorway.

I twisted in my seat to see Genevieve at the door, holding Finette's hand in her own. My heart broke at the sight of my beloved daughters. Genevieve had taken Finette under her wing, a second mother to my baby. Genevieve's black hair tumbled over her shoulders. Now that she was five, the pudgy babiness of her face and arms were starting to lengthen. A fair chance existed that she might end up as tall and lean as I.

Finette stood next to her, looking up to her sister in complete adoration. At three, her rich chestnut hair stuck out from her head in thin, baby-fine ringlets. A stockier child, taking after her father, but with such prettiness that any weight she might have when she was older wouldn't matter. My heart clenched in my chest as I gazed upon them. How beautiful my babies were.

"Come, *mes filles*. Maman is done with her papers. Shall we get ready for bed?"

Both girls cheered and clapped their hands. If I ever had to picture a moment of perfect joy, it was of their faces in this moment, excited to sleep in what Genevieve called "the big bed."

I took each of their hands and led them to my chambers, their animated voices escorting us down the hall. They had to tell me about each moment of the day:

"Maman, we got to pick peas today!"

"Maman, I petted a chick!"

"Maman, the cat chased a mouse but didn't catch it."

"Maman, we played in the hay!"

I nodded and smiled widely at them with every exclamation. Their conversation helped me forget my money woes.

We entered my room where the girls had left their night shifts that morning, on the end of the bed, ready for bedtime. I tugged and tugged, trying to fit Genevieve's head through her shift, and once it was on, it didn't reach her knees.

Genevieve looked at her shift. "Maman, I told you 'twas too small!"

"Yes, you did tell me. You shall wear it tonight, then we will wash it and give it to Finette. You would like a new shift, wouldn't you, Finette?"

I glanced over at her, and she lifted her middy shift to peek at me through a hole near the hem.

"And none too soon. You've worn holes in yours."

"Do we have money for a new shift, Maman?" Genevieve asked, adjusting her shift before turning to the bed. I sat up straight at her question.

"Where did you hear about money, Ginny?"

"I heard you tell the kitchen maid, Marie, that she had to leave our house because you didn't have the money."

Oh, little children had big ears. I blew a few wisps of loose hair off my face, then boosted Genevieve into the bed.

"Don't worry about money, Ginny. Your father left us plenty." I hate lying, but I wasn't going to have my five-year-old worrying about our finances. I lifted Finette into the bed where she curled into Genevieve.

"Oh, goody. I don't want us to not have money."

As the girls rested their head on the plush pillows, I changed out of my gown, my blue lawn that had started to show its wear a year ago, and put on my ragged shift. Tomorrow I'd search the house to see if we had any material I might use for a shift for Genevieve, then put my sewing skills to work.

As I blew out the candle, I tried not to think about what I should do if I didn't have any fabric. Not that linen was dear, it wasn't, but I needed every franc I had in that box.

The steady breathing of my daughters next to me lulled me to sleep.

I'd worry about Genevieve's shift on the morrow.

The main hall, the study, and the dining room had started to look empty. I'd sold the candle sticks, the rug in the dining room, most of the sliver, and a few pieces of art. The silver brought in the most, and from that, in addition to the upkeep of the manse, I was able to purchase some inexpensive fabric from the market to make dresses for the girls and myself.

Adele, who ran the fabric stall, had raised an eyebrow when I'd asked for the lesser expensive bolt of lawn fabric, but kept her thoughts to herself and took my money.

I'm sure rumors had started to fill the village and traveled all the way to Pointier about having to sell my husband's goods, but I didn't care. It paid for the house – that was the only thing I cared about.

My girls were ecstatic to have new dresses. I sewed theirs first and had them help with the stitching. With a patient hand, I showed Genevieve how to stitch the hem, how to put right sides together when sewing the dress together. Even Finette helped, collecting the extra scraps and putting them in the basket. I couldn't waste any of it, as I needed all of it to make three dresses, including one for my long frame. In moments such as this, I cursed my height. If I were short like the baker's wife, I'd need but half as much fabric for my gown.

With no money for the extra finery of lace or ribbon, the gowns were rather plain, but to Genevieve and Finette, their dresses were worthy of princesses. They pranced around the house and spun in dizzying circles as they held out their skirts.

Once my gown was finished, we dressed in our matching dresses and I brought out the larder basket. Filling it with old bread, fresh berries from the garden, and a few hard-boiled eggs, I treated the girls to a treat, a picnic in the broad expanse of grass not far from the main road.

We ate in the bright summer sunshine. Then the girls picked flowers and waved at travelers on the road. The girls chased butterflies as I shook out the blanket and led the girls home.

Much to my surprise, a stocky young man stood in the hall. My remaining maid, Jeanne, rushed to me when I entered, taking the basket from my hands.

"He says his name is Pierre Dubois. Andre's nephew."

My stomach fell to my feet. What was the nephew doing here? Was he no longer happy with the arrangement we had? Was he here to put my daughters and I out, making us homeless?

I tried to keep a calm expression on my face as I pushed the girls toward Jeanne.

"Jeanne, the girls are a bit dirty. Can you take them to the kitchen and clean them up, then take them to their room?"

I hoped I hid my nervousness from all of them. Jeanne nodded once, and with a wide smile, grasped Finette's fat little hand in her worn one.

"Come, lassies. Let's clean up and then find an activity in your room."

"Maman, who's that man?" Genevieve asked. The girl missed nothing.

"Just a visitor, lovey. Go with Jeanne and I will tell you about the man after he leaves."

Genevieve cut a wary gaze to the main hall before following Jeanne into the kitchens. I brushed my hand through my hair, hoping I didn't have any grass lingering in it. Then I took a deep breath and returned to the hall.

Then man's gray frock coat, warm for the day, pulled taut against his back. I could see it because he faced the fireplace, his hands clasped in front of him.

"Hello, *Monsieur* Dubois," I said to Andre's nephew in my nicest tone. "It is a pleasure to finally meet you."

"Where is the tapestry that hung over the mantle?" he asked without preface.

I inhaled, drawing myself up to my full height. I wasn't about to let this young man who'd abandoned us to our own devices intimidate me.

"I sold it. Since I've had no money coming in, I needed to support the house somehow."

I left the implication hanging in the air — *since you didn't help support us.*

"I've heard. I've heard you've had to sell several items. I will not have you selling my family heirlooms."

"They are also my daughter's heirlooms, Andre's daughter's heirlooms. But feeding his daughter is more important than a shining candlestick or a pretty tapestry."

"Or a pretty gown?" His gray gaze roved over my dress, and I ignored the statement. He knew nothing of our predicament. "It brings out your eyes."

I didn't react to his odd compliment. At the moment, hatred for the man boiled under my skin.

Pierre turned back to the mantle, resting one short arm on it. He kept his gaze averted from me as he spoke. Coward.

"You are on the verge of being destitute. You have no place for your daughters, and I've heard that your parents are in no place to take you in since your father has died. Financially you have nothing."

I despised this man, not only for his position in Andre's family, but for pointing out the harsh truth I had tried to dismiss. Having one's dire situation stated so plainly was painful.

"Yet, you are still young and very beautiful. Childbirth didn't take from you as it does other women. In that, you are fortunate, as I have a solution to your problem."

My problem? He was my problem! And what possible solution could he have?

"There is someone I'd like you to meet."

Not again! I vowed never to be sold off to another man, no matter how destitute I was! If I were to wed again, it would be for a love match. This I vowed to myself.

I didn't tell Pierre any of this. What care would he have for my desires? He just wanted his house and belongings to remain intact – which wasn't going to happen if I had to sell off those belongings. He cared nothing for us. He was the type of man who wanted his family's wealth for himself alone.

"Monsieur, I believe you overstep." My voice was harsh, biting.

"Non, I don't believe I do. You cannot maintain this house, this lifestyle for your daughters. I have a friend, a lord with a profitable bit of land on the west side of Pointiers, whom is in need of a wife. He doesn't seem to think so, but I disagree."

Ugh. Another old man. That was not going to happen again, I promised myself.

"I am not about to wed a man I've never met."

Pierre turned to me and nodded. "That is fair. You had at least met my uncle a few times before you wed. This man is not like my uncle. He is younger, to start. His wealth is comparable, if not greater. And he had a daughter already, one that is near the ages of yours, if I don't miss my guess."

Pierre could argue convincingly, I had to give him that. But I still wasn't going to marry a man I didn't know, even if he was younger and wealthy.

"His name is Seigneur Luc Fournier. His daughter is Ella. He is passing this way later in the week, and I'd like to invite him to dinner here. Then you can meet him and make your decision."

I leveled my gaze at Pierre. I hated how he could demand, and I had to obey. Invite a man I didn't know to dinner in my own home. In my dead husband's home? It seemed inappropriate. Pierre didn't seem to care.

"Do I have a choice?" I asked.

Pierre didn't hesitate. "*Non.*"

I finally dropped my gaze. I was going to be sold off again.

Chapter Five

PIERRE ARRIVED EARLY, looking quite the foppish man, his belly pressing against his too-tight shirt. His plain brown hair was slicked over to the side, and not for the first time, I wondered if he tried to cover the beginnings of a bald spot.

He had been thoughtful enough to send in a cook and servers earlier in the day, and the house sagged under the heady scents of lamb, apples, and yeasty bread. The girls peeked their tiny faces around the kitchen door frame, watching the activity in the kitchen as though it were a pageant.

I fed them first, lean slices of lamb with roasted apples, potatoes dripping in butter, and caramelized pears for dessert. They hadn't eaten so richly in a long while. With happy bellies and sticky faces, I sent them upstairs with Jeanne, under strict orders to get cleaned up and ready for bed, and not come back downstairs.

Only then did I begin to ready myself.

I sat at my vanity table, studying myself in the chipped glass. Pierre spoke the truth. My black hair was still long and shiny. I made sure to brush it out every night, and the locks flowed down my back in a black velvet river. My gray-green eyes were yet clear and unwrinkled, as was my brow. I touched a bit of rouge to my cheeks to give my pale pallor a bit of color and then turned to my wardrobe.

I still had all the gowns Andre had gifted me years ago, and a few others I'd acquired while married, but most were looking their age, worn with loose threads or stains or thinning fabric. My gold and blue brocade was the best of the bunch, as I'd had but few scant occasions to wear it, and without the help of Jeanne, I struggled to get into it and lace up the front. The gold braid was still bright, and when I cinched the bodice against my kirtle, my breasts lifted nicely, showcasing that they, too, were just as smooth and inviting as when I was young.

Several pins and a gold braid snood for my hair, and when I looked in the glass again, the vision that peered back was the vision of French society, a catch for any man.

I sighed heavily. Why was I trying so hard? I should wear the tattered, striped lawn and my apron and let this important man see that.

But I also knew that if I didn't manage to captivate this rich lord, then my daughters would end up destitute. I'd do anything for them, even sell my soul to the devil.

And that devil was named Pierre.

I heard Pierre's knock at the door and slipped on my plain brown slippers — there was nothing to be done for those except hope my skirts covered them for the night. I had no other shoes.

Pierre settled into an overstuffed chair near the hearth as I swept into the kitchens, the full lady of the manor, to check on the food. The servants had set an exquisite table, complete with bright embroidered linens, silver chargers and delicate porcelain dishes that matched the chargers and linens. Silver candlesticks sat at both ends of the table, and a bouquet of spring wildflowers in a low silver bowl served as the centerpiece. Truly, the dining room had not looked so fine in years.

Another knock at the door, and this time my heart fell to my feet. This was it — time to meet the man who'd change my future. I knew nothing of him other than his name, Luc Fournier, and I had to hope he was kind on the eyes. Or at least younger than my previous husband.

When I stepped into the main hall, Pierre swiveled on his heel and held out an arm to me.

When the man walked into the room, I was struck immediately by his tall lean frame and shock of tawny blondish hair that fell in gentle waves to his collar curling slightly against the fabric. A hint of ruffles peeked from his coat cuffs and at his collar, which showcased the hard edge of his jaw. His rich burgundy velvet surcoat fit him perfectly, showcasing his long, strong arms. Long in both leg and body, his slender build hinted at raw, lean-muscled power.

I couldn't believe it. *This?* This was Luc Fournier? Seigneur Fournier of Nouâtre? Surely, there had to be a mistake. Men like him, as handsome and this powerful and supposedly as wealthy as Pierre suggested, did not walk into my life. They didn't saunter into my salon because they were looking for a wife. Surely this had to be a mistake.

It was his eyes, though, that stopped me, held me fixed to my place on the rug. His eyes were a rich wine, and I felt as though I could get drunk on his gaze. They weren't quite blue, not quite green, brighter than the river depths on a sunlit summer day. And like a summer day, his eyes held me in their warmth. I couldn't focus on anything else, not even when this fine man reached for my hand and bent low to kiss it. Only when he broke his gaze did I regain my wits.

"Corrine, it is my pleasure to introduce you to *Seigneur* Fournier. *Monsieur* Fournier, I present to you Corrine Dubois." I didn't miss the self-satisfied smile that Pierre tried ineffectually to hide.

Luc's eyes never left me, and I started to sweat uncomfortable droplets rolling down the small of my back under my corseted frock. The way he looked at me had an intensity that rivaled a thousand suns, and I wondered if his tempting gaze made me feel this way. What would it be like to be married to this man, share a bed with this man?

"Madame, the pleasure is all mine," Luc said in a deep voice that rumbled through the room. His voice was smooth, a rich baritone that vibrated in my chest. He didn't release my hand, but stood there sharing my gaze, holding my hand in his warm, calloused one. *A lord who worked?* I wondered.

I allowed myself to melt into his hand. And I wondered what he was hiding from me. There had to be something else, something about this man that Pierre wasn't telling me, because men like this just did not walk into my world.

A nudge at my side distracted me, and I turned to see Pierre thrusting a sharp elbow into my ribs. Pierre cleared his throat, interrupting the moment. I had yet to speak a word to Luc, and Pierre was reminding me of my manners.

"Monsieur Fournier, you do flatter me. Welcome to Château Dubois."

Luke lifted my hand to his lips and kissed it, the gentle pressure of his lips burning into my skin marking me as his and my mind spun. I was dizzy from the very presence of Luc. Pierre spoke up, breaking the heightened illustrious tension in the room.

"The servants have dinner on the table. Why don't we retire to the dining room?"

Luc kept my hand in his and gave me a tight smile before following me into the dining room. I didn't know if it was just the collection of the fine dishes and linens or if it was the glaze in my eyes, but just having Luc in the dining room made the entire room brighter and exciting.

As the servants served our soup, a creamed crab ragout, Luc asked me about my life at Château Dubois, marveled over the antics of my children, and opened up about his personal life.

"Pierre mentioned that you live here alone with your daughters. How do you manage?"

He could be making small talk, but from his tone, he sounded genuinely interested.

"We have a small garden off the kitchens, and the animals provide us with meat, milk, eggs, and cheese. We are fortunate."

It was then that I learned more about his daughter. From his description, she was a blonde doll who missed her departed mother very much.

Her mother died when Elle was but three, Luc explained. I raised a sleek black eyebrow at him. Was that it? Was that the big secret, the formidable mystery that made *Monsieur* Fournier somehow less desirable as a husband? I couldn't imagine such a thing. Men had children all the time and still made fine matches with noble women. Surely, it had to be something other than a poor, motherless daughter that kept him from finding another wife.

"My dedication to her," Luc continued, "has kept me close to home. It is only as of late, as Ella is becoming a young woman, that I thought it prudent she have a mother."

At first, I didn't know what to say to his thoughtful answer. Was he interested in me because of my status as a mother? That was my sole value? But before that line of thought could progress further, he continued.

"And in truth, my loneliness has started to hang about me in a painful cloak. If I am to be a good father to my daughter, I must be a good man. And a man of stature can only truly be a good man if he has a wife."

Pierre burst out with the laughter at Luc's comment, and Luc's cheeks brightened with pink roses, very flattering on the man, in my humble opinion. I glared at Pierre for laughing at Luc who was exposing his heart to me. In an effort to silence him, I lifted my foot under the table and kicked him. He scowled and snapped his jaw shut.

"Why *Monsieur* Fournier," I tried to temper Pierre's inappropriate laughter, "I don't think I've ever heard such beauty pour from a man's lips."

If anything, Luc blushed all the more.

"Well, I thank you, milady. It's kind of you to say. And what of you? You say you are well established here at Château Dubois. What is it that you seek in a husband?"

It took every ounce of my willpower not to flash another glare at Pierre. Perchance once I got to know Luc, and we did marry, I'd be free to open up to him about the stingy nature of Pierre and now he was driving me from my home. At the moment, however, I didn't know Luc that well, and it seemed imprudent to make such a claim in front of Pierre himself.

"I, too, have need of a husband, just as you have need of a wife."

At this, Luc smiled widely, and I fairly swooned in my seat. He had a dimple. A tiny, barely noticeable dimple that peeked out when his face effused with joy. And that dimple *winked* at me.

In that moment, I believed in God as I had the day my babies were born. Sometimes life worked in such a way to lead us to a point in life where we are supposed to be.

All the trauma, all the misery in my life had led me to this point where I could meet Luc.

I knew deep in my heart that my life would never be the same.

The more he spoke, the more his words took my breath away. Luc spoke eloquently, from the heart, even in front of Pierre, who seemed to hang on every word. I sent Pierre a cutting look, not my first of the night, but the man didn't care. Instead, he ogled at us in our dinner conversation as though we were colorful, exotic animals.

But I didn't take note. Every word that fell from Luc's lips was the sweetest wine, and I was getting drunk off him. I rudely placed my elbow on the table and sunk my chin into the palm of my hand. By the time the roast leg of lamb arrived, I believed I was in love.

That thought snapped me back to attention, and I straightened, dropping my gaze to my hands. He said he wanted a wife, but he didn't say *me*! Oh, the audacity I had, to presume so much from one meeting.

The servant placed my lamb on my plate. I reached for my silverware, but I couldn't raise my face.

"Are you well?" Luc said suddenly. His hand breached the chasm of the dining room table and covered my hand. Caring. Protective. A touch unlike any I'd felt in my life. My God, how could anyone *not* love him?

"*Oui*, my apologies. I fear I may have over indulged in the ragout."

I withdrew my other hand, the one he wasn't touching, and held my stomach as I feign my digestive complaint. From the corner of my eye, I could see Pierre scowling at my abrupt change in disposition. If I were a different woman, a younger woman, I might have stuck my tongue out at him.

"Oh, dear. I regret that this dinner must end soon. Perchance I might call you again? Later in the week, if that is agreeable?"

Oh, that earnest voice. I risked raising my gaze and his eyes bore into me as earnestly as his voice spoke. He wanted to see me again? I hadn't been overreacting to Luc's presence?

I nodded. *"Oui,* I would like that. On Fridays, we have beef . . ." I trailed off as Luc patted my hand.

"No, I insist. You must come to my chateau. I'll have the chef prepare *Bœuf Bourgignon,* and if you like, you can bring your daughters. They can meet my Ella. If we are so well met, shouldn't we make sure the children are?"

My breath caught in my chest and I was frozen in my spot. He thought we were well met? He wanted our children to meet? Did that mean . . .?

Pierre couldn't control himself, the lout.

"Oh, that sounds like a fine idea, *Seigneur* Luc. Should I accompany you, perchance to chaperon?"

If I hadn't loved Luc before now, then the look he gave Pierre would have won my heart over. Luc peered down his nose at Pierre, physically down his nose, and in the most condescending air I ever heard, he spoke.

"I rather believe three young children should be sufficient escorts. Don't you agree, Pierre?"

Oh! The use of Pierre's first name after Pierre had formally addressed Luc all evening had to strike a chord. Pierre crinkled his lip, then replaced it with that fake looking smile.

"Of course. Three young ladies are assuredly enough to chaperon."

An unladylike snort escaped me, but I couldn't help myself. Pierre had probably been looking forward to a free, elegant meal after the expense of this one. Luc's flirtatious eyes caught mine, and we shared a smile, as though we were both in on the same joke. His fingers lingered on my hand, a warm, dizzying weight.

And something inside me knew that I'd have that touch, that weight, forever.

After Pierre ushered Luc to the door and followed him out to leave, I breathed a giant sigh of relief, blowing loose wisps of my back hair from my face. I leaned against the dining room door. My heart hadn't stopped fluttering the entire night, and the single imperfection was the moment Luc's hand left mine.

I watched as he flexed it several times before resting it under the table. As though he was shocked at the feeling in his fingers. Maybe they flexed in thinking of what else he might touch. I smiled at that. Yes, I'd very much like Luc to touch me again.

Placing a light hand under my up-thrust bosom, I took several deep breaths, trying to get control of myself before heading upstairs. In my current state, I'd never fall asleep.

I peeked in on my girls before approaching my bedroom. Since I didn't go right to bed, the maid had settled them in their tiny beds. I gazed at them, my hearts tucked into embroidered quilts, when Finette's serious little eye peeked open.

"Are they gone? Can we come to your bed?" she whispered loudly enough for her sister to stir. I held a finger to my lips.

"You are already tucked in. Surely you don't want to stay here?"

Finette, so willful, shook her head. Guinevere finally awoke enough to join in on the pleading.

"Is it time for bed, Maman?" she also whispered.

I chewed at my lips. I should keep them in their beds. If I married Luc, they'd no longer be able to sleep with me. I should start preparing them for that now.

At the same time, another voice in my head pointed out that, if I wed, they'd no longer sleep with me, so I better take advantage of that time whilst I had it. That voice won.

"Come," I said, waggling my hand at them. "To bed then."

The girls scrambled from their low beds and joined me. As usual, though they were tired, their questions were not.

"Why are you dressed so pretty, Maman?" Finette asked.

"Do you think I look pretty?" I countered.

"You look beautiful, Maman!" Guinevere confirmed. "Was it because of the men who visited? Who were they?"

Ahh, my ever-astute Guinevere. How was I to share this news? I wracked my brain, trying to find the best words to frame the events of the night.

"You remember how I told you that we don't own this house? That your uncle Pierre does?"

The girls nodded in unison. We were in my bedroom, and I boosted them into the high bed. They cuddled under the covers to listen to me talk as I undressed for bed.

"Well, the upkeep of the house is expensive. And it's not fit for a woman like myself to live alone. Or for such beautiful girls as you not to have a father. Your uncle Pierre is trying to rectify that by introducing me to a man of means who is looking for a wife."

There I said it and as I unlaced my gown and peeled it off with a breath of relief, my girls' eyes grew wider than the soup bowls from supper.

"A father? You are going to have a new husband? Not Father?"

Guinevere's voice was tight. Was she worried? Upset? Angry? She could hide her emotions when she wanted to, that one. Finette was easier — her tiny face screwed up in a giant question mark. She didn't much recall Andre, and the concept of a father was lost on her. Poor thing.

"Maybe. I'm not sure yet. This is a big decision, and I won't make it lightly. I need to ensure that this is the best for all of us, not just me. So, this Friday, we are going to his estate for dinner. He has a daughter, just your ages, and you will get to meet her."

Guinevere sat up at this development and clasped her hands under her chin. "A new friend? I like her already! What is her name?"

My heart ached at the impassioned joy Guinevere had at the idea of making a new friend. She was a friend to every living thing at the chateau. Of course, she'd be ecstatic. Finette appeared cautious but followed her sister's lean and also clapped excitedly.

"Ella. Her name is Ella, and she's had no mother for most of her life. Only her father. We think this might be a good match. Are you comfortable meeting her and her father?"

"Oh, *oui,* Maman!" She clapped again. "And what is his name?"

I finished pulling on my sleeping shift and climbed into bed. Settling between my girls, I wrapped an arm around each of them.

"Luc. Luc Fournier."

The girls quieted, snuggled into me. They seemed pleased, and I dearly hoped they were. Then Guinevere spoke up again.

"You looked happy tonight, Maman. Does he make you happy?"

Her eyes were still bright in the darkened room. My mind relived the sensation of Luc touching my hand, and my skin tingled where his fingers had rested.

"Oui, I rather believe he does," I told her.

She tucked her head into me and closed her eyes.

"Then I like him, Maman."

Chapter Six

I DRESSED US in our finest dresses for our dinner with Luc.

That gracious and thoughtful man had sent a light oak carriage with padded velvet seats to retrieve us, and we rode in luxury to Chateau Fournier. The girls giggled with delight the whole way.

Chateau Fournier was a marvel to behold. Even my excitable daughters grew silent as we pulled into the overhang of the *porte cochere*. The Chateau rivaled a palace in my mind, not having ever seen one. The manse had to be three stories tall, with the roof narrowing to sharp peaks. Several of those topmost windows were stained glass, the type I thought only existed in churches.

The footman helped my girls jump down from the carriage, but when I extended my hand and ducked my head out of the carriage, it wasn't the footman who stood ready to help me step to the cobblestone path, but my future husband. His hand was as warm and welcoming as the smile on his handsome face.

"Welcome to Chateau Fournier, milady. We are pleased to have you in our home."

I don't know if he noticed, but my cheeks heated with a hard blush. He threaded my arm through his as I balanced myself on the cobblestones, then escorted me into the manse. The warmth of his body radiated through his coat and made me warmer than I already was.

"Thank you for having us," I answered as we walked, trying to remember my manners.

We reached the open door, and a silhouette of a little girl stood in the doorway.

Ella.

Luc hadn't exaggerated. She did resemble a doll, with puckered pink lips, loose golden curls, and dressed in a delicate, ruffled dress that touched the top of her brown buckles.

Her eyes, though, I wasn't ready for her eyes. Instead of kind eyes, they were hard, angry, the sparkling blue lost in her fury.

"Darling Ella, please meet Madame Dubois and her daughters, Genevieve and Finette."

Each of my girls performed a well-mannered curtsy, and a swell of pride filled my chest. Ella, however, didn't curtsy back. Rather, her face hardened.

"I don't want them here, Father," she said in a tone shockingly sharp for so tiny a girl.

Genevieve and Finette didn't know what to do and looked up at me for guidance. Luc stiffened, ready to have his sharp words with her, but I laid a hand on his arm and stepped forward and crouched to Ella's level.

"*Bon soir*, Ella. I know this must be a bit hard for you, but I have heard so much about you. I am pleased to meet you. Can you get to know us tonight?"

I kept my voice light, tender, just as when I spoke to my girls when they struggled with their childhood emotions. Nothing. No response, no softening of her hard features. Ella spun and ran away, probably to her room.

"Ella!" Luc thundered. I stood and placed my hand on his brawny chest.

"No, Monsieur Fournier, let her run. This is hard for her, and she's just a child. She doesn't know what to do or how he to deal with these changes. Have her come down to dinner after she's had the chance to calm herself."

Luc bowed his fair head at me. "As always, I shall defer to your greater patience. I am blessed to have a woman such as you in my home."

His words were full of heady emotion, as emotional as his daughter's behavior, I surmised, and it seemed he might have meant something other than this visit in this moment. Was he considering marriage? Was he that convinced?

Was I? As we entered, I admired the robust beauty of his home, my thoughts were not fully focused on the rooms he showed with pride. I didn't want to believe in love at first sight, but it seemed that Luc had fallen victim to Cupid's arrow.

He swept me away with his kind words and thoughtful actions when he had dinner at Chateau Dubois, but the past two days gave me time to reflect. I wanted to say I fell in love with him at that dinner, but I was jaded. I didn't want to believe that one could fall in love that quickly with someone they had just met.

But the past days hadn't calmed the quivering in my chest or weakness in my knees when I thought about him. There was an excellent chance I'd fallen for him.

I flicked my eyes at him as he showed me his study, done in rich woods and towering bookcases that reached the rafters. His loving, leaf-green eyes weren't focused on his prized possessions.

They were on me.

Maybe it was love at first sight for Luc.

And deep inside, I really hoped it was.

Ella did join us for dinner, pouting the entire time. I tried not to be disappointed, but I had so hoped she'd like me, like Genevieve and Finette, to see her sulking did damper my exuberance a bit.

I didn't let that hinder me at all. I still smiled at her throughout dinner, tried to engage her in childlike conversation and pressed my girls to do the same. I was determined for her to love us, just as I wanted to love her. For Luc, if for nothing else.

Luc. At that dinner he was a model of manly perfection. Refined without being foppish like Pierre, good-natured, funny, and his eyes . . . Oh, those eyes! What was it about how he looked at me, those fiery eyes that burned right through me to my core? Like there was nothing else in this room, in this world, other than me. I shivered every time he shifted his eyes in my direction.

Ella might have noticed, for she seemed to pout harder when Luc was distracted by me. I didn't pay her behavior any mind. She was just a little girl and jealous that someone might take her father away. As soon as she realized I was going to help keep him here with her, she'd start to warm to me.

Genevieve and Finette were all dimpled smiles as we poured back into the carriage. Ella stood next to Luc, her tiny hand wrapped in his, and she glared at me when he kissed my hand goodbye. I wanted his lips, but he was too proper to act on those base desires, especially in front of wee Ella.

I turned to walk the short distance on those cobblestones, now hard to see in the dark of night, when Luc tugged on my hand, urging me back. He let go of Ella's hand, her scowl deepening in return, and reached into his pocket.

Before I understood what was going on, he held out a ring, a beautiful emerald and gold piece that glittered as a star falling from the sky. I gasped, my mind reeling.

What was he about?

"Corinne." His voice wavered as he said my name – strong, confident Luc's voice was wavering? "In the short time I have known you, I cannot stop thinking of you. I think we are well-met, that our daughters will get along with time, and in truth, you consume my days. I can think of nothing I want more than to spend the rest of those days with you. Will you consider becoming Madame de Fournier, my wife?"

His strong fingers held the ring out, a tentative offering, as though I could say *no*! Even with Ella practically spitting and whining next to him, how could any woman deny this man?

"*Oui*, Monsieur Fournier," I whispered, extending my fingers to him so he might slide the ring on. "'Twould be my honor." My voice wavered, too.

"I think now is the time when you should start calling me Luc," he whispered in a heady voice, my hand still warm in his.

"Kiss her already!" A high-pitched, giggling squeal called from the carriage. I flipped my black locks over my shoulder to see Genevieve and Finette leaning out the carriage window. Of course, Genevieve made her voice heard.

Luc raised one eyebrow at me, and I gave a light nod. He leaned into me, his lips brushing lightly, sending shivers down my spine. Then his arms slipped around my waist, drawing me closer, and he deepened the kiss, his urgency readily apparent. The girls giggled behind me.

He released me, and I patted my hands against the soft fabric of his coat.

"You will have to move in. You can stay in the guest quarters until we wed. I'll send a carriage for you and your belongings tomorrow. "

His voice left no option to question his command, and I stepped into the carriage and blew him a kiss from the window. Luc remained illuminated in the doorway until we could no longer see the entry.

It wasn't until we were nearly home that I realized I hadn't seen Ella standing next to him.

Chapter Seven

THE HEAVENS THEMSELVES must have blessed my wedding day to Luc, for it dawned brightly, with the tittering of Ortolan songbirds waking me. My girls and I were staying in the guest quarters of Chateau Fournier, at the behest of Luc, and when I opened my eyes to the creamy chiffon gown hanging from the wardrobe, I thought I must still be in a dream.

Luc's generosity had bordered on madness. Once he realized the less-than-desirable living situation at Chateau Dubois, he acted quickly, offering me and my girls the guest house and moving our belongings into what would eventually be our rooms. I had protested, of course, claiming it was far too much, but Luc disagreed. He'd patted my hand and kissed my cheek and told me it was his pleasure.

How had my life changed so dramatically, so wonderfully, in so short a time?

I rose from the cool bedding and strode to the wardrobe, caressing the gown again. How many times had I let my fingers linger on the fabric over the past few days? I had lost count.

The sunrise-hued gown itself was high-waisted, with a jewel encrusted ribbon secured just below her breasts. The bodice had soft folded pleats to enhance my bosom, and a slip of a sleeve designed to sit at the tops of my arms. The skirt fell long to the floor, and a sheer panel hung from my back and around my hips, then trailed behind me in a train. Luc had even commissioned a slender, sparkling tiara that matched the glittering waistband ribbon.

But the gift that had truly marveled me, the gift that seemed almost impossible and left me speechless, had been wrapped in what I thought was a hatbox.

Why did he gift me a hat when he'd already given me the tiara?

"This took a bit longer to craft," he'd explained, sitting on the edge of his seat like an excited little boy. His verdant eyes sparkled. In my mind, I could see the son we'd have one day in his face.

The ribbon was delicate, no more than a wisp of fabric, and I had tugged gently to unwrap yet another thoughtful gift. When I lifted the lid, I'd had to take a moment to understand what I was seeing.

They were shoes, but unlike any shoe I'd ever laid eyes on. Reaching into the padded box, I'd extracted the glinting heels. A low heel, not too high, but how could it be high when it was made of glass?

Surely my eyes deceive me. Shoes can't be glass!

I had lifted out the other shoe, my sapphire eyes as wide as the sky. What magic were these shoes?

"Do you like them?" Luc's eager voice had asked.

"Are they made of glass?" I had needed confirmation. I couldn't believe my eyes.

"Yes. I had them specially crafted to your foot size. The cobbler had to work with the glass smith, and both had said they'd never heard of such a thing. But I wanted everything you wore on your wedding day to be as refined and beautiful as you. The shoes, they don't even come close," he had said, studying my eyes with an intensity that made my heart skip in my chest.

Then he had leaned over the box and caught my lips in his. A soft, pre-wedding kiss, one that gained slow pressure and promised a fulfilled future. I had sighed into that kiss.

Luc had sat back suddenly, cleaning his throat and adjusting his coat.

"Um, so, will they fit?"

I had set the box on the floor and reached down to slip off my leather slippers. Luc had extended his hands and took the glass slippers from me.

"May I?" he had asked, tilting his head toward her feet. I had giggled. He'd wanted to put the shoes on me. What manner of man was he? An impossible one. I had poked my bare feet out from under my skirts and Luc had bent on one knee, and with the most exquisite precision, he cupped one foot in his hand and slipped it on my foot. He'd then done the same with the other, and my feet looked like something from a fairy story. Had any princess in history had more beautiful feet? I didn't think so.

"They're beautiful," I'd marveled.

"The pale in comparison to you," Luc had responded. And if possible, I'd fallen even more in love with him.

Those shoes now sat nestled in the box next to the wardrobe. I hadn't shown the girls yet; I wanted them to be surprised.

Genevieve and Finette, they'd fawn over the elegant shoes. I kept my hand on my gown, lost in my thoughts.

Ella, she would be another matter. I bit at my lip.

It had but been a few days since they'd met, hardly enough time to get to know the wee girl, but I prayed that the girl's deportment toward my daughters and me changed over time.

Just the night before, Ella had kicked Finette, poor, tiny Finette! And the child didn't know how to respond, so she just burst into tears at the assault. Both Genevieve and I came running to her aid. Genevieve had arrived first, and Ella pushed her away!

I'd have chastised my own girls harshly, but this poor girl, she had no one. No sister to come to her aid as Finette did, no mother as her girls had. So instead of reprimanding the girl, I had knelt between

Ella and Finette. Then I patted Finette, telling she was fine and to go with her sister. Turning my gaze upon Ella, I had taken the girl's tiny hands in my own. Ella's watery blue eyes had narrowed, slinging hatred at me, and I ignored it as the look of a lost, sad child.

"Oh, Ella," I had said in her gentlest tone. "I know this is much for you, and sudden. But we only want the best for you. To be sisters and a mother that you don't have. We just want to love you."

Ella's face had closed at my words. "You are not my mother," Ella had spat out.

I nodded. "Of course, Ella. I can never replace her. But I can try to fill that role for you know, to be a friend and a confidant as needed. Genevieve and Finette already want to love you as a sister. They can be your closest allies if you let them. I can, too. I love you already, and I want the best for you."

Ella's dear eyes had filled, and she had torn her watery gaze from me and ran to her room.

I had placed her hands on her knees and watched her run, the frilly lilac Polonaise of her dress flapping at her heels. Then I'd risen and found Genevieve and Finette. Finette's tears had dried, but her face was yet a mask of sadness.

"Maman, I didn't mean to make her angry. I just wanted to play," Finette had cried. I sat between the two girls and put an arm around them each.

"I know, *ma fille*. But she's sad right now. Her father is all she has, and she sees us as taking him away from her. We must forgive these behaviors and love her even when she is unlovable. That is when she needs it the most. Can we do that?"

My girls had leaned into me. "Of course, we can, Maman," Genevieve told me with authority.

I had hugged them tighter. "What good girls you are. And one day she will love us all. We just need to be patient."

My heart still was pained that morning, just thinking about Ella's behavior the night before. I knew deep in my heart that, as loving a man as Luc was, some of that had to be in Ella, and if we just gave her time, she might feel loved, feel part of this growing family.

For now, I hoped my girls had enough patience until that happened.

A knock at the door drew me from my thoughts and the softness of the gown.

"Maman? Are you awake? Jeanne said we could see you," Genevieve's voice was little more than a whisper.

"Of course! Come in, my sweet!" Genevieve rushed in, followed by Finette, and they scrambled barefoot to me. Seeing the glittery gown and tiara, they stopped short.

"Maman! It's so beautiful! You'll look like a princess!"

I smiled sweetly at my awe-stricken daughters. "Wait until you see these."

Then I reached for the box and lifted the lid. The shoes caught a shaft of early morning light and scattered rainbows around the room. Their mouths fell open and my chatty girls fell silent.

"Maman," Genevieve whispered quieter than when she was in church, "what are these?"

"I'm not sure, but they are glass slippers. I am to wear them today."

Finette moved her hands as if to touch them, then yanked her hands back.

"Would you like to try them on?"

Both girls squealed and clapped their hands, and I told them to sit on the bed. Taking a shoe in each hand, I put one on Genevieve's foot and the other on Finette's. The shoes hung off their tiny feet, but they lifted their legs and admired the glittery glass shoes.

"And one day," I told them with pride and joy in my voice, "as you are my daughters, you shall wear these on your wedding day."

"Oh, Maman!" Finette clasped her hands under her chin. Her face shone almost as bright as the sun.

Genevieve's smile faltered. "Maman, if Ella is to become your daughter, will she wear these one day, too?"

I crouched in front of my girls and placed a hand on each girl's knee. "*Oui*, today she becomes my daughter just as you are, and if she desires to wear these shoes, then I will gladly let her." I flicked my gaze between them. I could hope they recalled our conversation about Ella from the night before. "Is that acceptable to you?"

Finette looked to Genevieve to answer — always ready to follow her sister's lead.

Genevieve studied her glass-enclosed foot, then nodded slowly. "*Oui*, Maman. You are right. She is becoming our sister, your daughter, and she deserves to wear something this beautiful on her wedding day, just as we do."

My heart swelled, and tears clouded my eyes. I was so full of love that day, full to bursting, and their thoughtfulness threatened to push me over the edge. I slipped the glass shoes off their feet and set them in the box.

Standing swiftly, I wiped my eyes on my sleeve and moved to the door.

"We have a busy day ahead of us. Shall we see if Jeanne has breakfast ready?"

The girls climbed from the bed and raced to the door.

They were just as excited to start this day as I was.

Chapter Eight

LUC HAD SENT a carriage for my mother, my father having passed a few years before, and she grinned without end upon arrival. A footman in a dark blue coat with shiny brass buttons held her hand as she stepped down from the white carriage, as if my mother were royalty. And she lifted her head high and threw her shoulders back, feeling like royalty. Watching from my high window, I watched her waddle toward the garden and grinned to myself. She was overjoyed at this wedding, and I was secure knowing that Luc had offered to help pay for my mother's upkeep. He was generous to a fault.

My girls' gowns for the day resembled mine, more yellow than cream. Jeanne and the new governess, Margaux Renaud, had helped fashion their hair in ribbons and the girls felt so grown up, prancing about the yard.

Luc had hired a lady's maid for me, and she worked wonders with my hair and tiara, so the gem-encrusted tiara surrounded a crown of ebony black curls, and the rest fell in waves over my shoulders, under the film of veil crafted of the same translucent material as the panels on my gown. When she showed me the final look in the reflecting glass, I gasped. I didn't recognize myself. How had I managed to come so far? To end up in this princess life after so much strife.

I blinked back tears as my maid helped fit my feet into the glass slippers.

"I have never seen the like, milady. They are extraordinary," she said with reverence.

"Thank you, Anne. I agree. They were a gift from Luc."

"You are fortunate in him, and he in you, I believe," Anne commented with a slight curtsy. I beamed impossibly wider.

"Thank you again. Why don't you go finish getting yourself ready and join the guests in the garden? I will be down shortly."

"You don't need my help?"

"I can walk just fine, even in these glass shoes. Now go. I'll see you down there."

I shooed her off with a smile, and she graciously bowed again before leaving.

Now it was time for me to take a breath, ready myself for this moment, and calm my nerves. I sipped at my tepid tea, taking care not to spill a drop and ruin this gown. Nothing could ruin this day.

When I stepped into the hallway, I descended the curving stairway, holding onto the carved stair rail so as not to trip on the hem of the dress. I had just reached the bottom when Ella raced in, heading toward the back door to the garden.

She wasn't in her wedding day gown.

Ella stopped short and glared at me.

"Why didn't you wear your wedding day gown, Ella?" I asked with as much tenderness as I could muster. I wouldn't let Ella's sour attitude ruin my day, but I wanted her to have a good day as well. Why couldn't she at least try?

"My father bought you those clothes," she bit out.

What? She was mad her father purchased my wedding finery?

I pressed my fingers against the bridge of my nose and reminded myself that it wasn't the clothing, the gown, the shoes. It was a sad little girl who missed her mother and was afraid of losing her father. And she had new people forced into her life. She was too young to understand how truly good this was for her, and she was lashing out.

I was the adult, and from seeing my girls struggle with their father's death and our uncertainty at Chateau Dubois, I understood what she was doing. Instead of getting angry, which is what I really wanted to do, I crouched low, balancing as best I could in my glass slippers, so I was at her level.

"Oui. Your father is more than generous, and I love him dearly for that. And I love you. I am so excited to be a part of your family and have you as another daughter. Will you walk with me to the gardens?"

I stood and held my hand out to her, thinking that perchance my words might have broken through her hard shell.

Ella moved toward me, and my smile was so wide I thought it'd split my face in two.

Then she lifted a foot and kicked me square in the shin. With a final stink eye at me, she ran out the door toward the gardens.

I rubbed my leg, more shocked than in pain. But that wasn't the worst. Her shoe was a soft leather slipper, so the kick didn't hurt much at all. Her shoe was filthy, just as much of the girl often was (*I'll have to encourage her to play less in the dirt and cinders after we settle into the household,* I told myself), and a horseshoe-like dirt mark stained the gossamer skirts.

"Ella!" I screeched, inhaling sharply. I wiped my hand over the stain, hoping to wipe away most of it. A light brown shadow of the kick remained, no matter how hard I wiped.

She's just a little girl, I reminded myself over and over as I blinked back the tears that threatened to fall. I patted my cheeks quickly, trying to stop the tears. I wasn't going to cry on my wedding day. This day was a dream come true, and I vowed not to let this child ruin it for me.

"Madame! What are you still doing here? Everyone awaits you in the garden!"

The squeaky voice behind me caught me by surprise and I jumped in my delicate shoes and wobbled until I could balance myself again. I turned to find Margaux behind me, looking as fine as she might in a yellow and brown gown, the fitted bodice nearly busting against her large bosom. Her graying brown hair was pulled high on her head and flattered her rounded face.

"Margaux! You frightened me!"

"Oh, Madame. Why are you dawdling? And did I see Ella here? Is she with you?"

"Um, well, no. She's not very happy, I think."

"And is that dirt on your gown?" Margaux pointed. "What happened?"

"Just a bit of a run in with Ella, I'm afraid."

I didn't want to complain about the girl, but I needed to unload on someone. Margaux was that someone.

"Well, she is trying to deal with having a crowd of people move into her house, change all she's known for her life, and her father now spending time with you. Children do adapt though. Ella will come around soon enough."

I tried not to narrow my eyes at Margaux's words as she held the door to the garden open wide for me. It wasn't what she said – I had already come to the same conclusions about Ella. It was how she said them. Despite myself, I had to bite back, assert my authority as the new lady of the house.

"Yes, that I know from having two daughters of my own. But it's a change for all of us. My daughters are being taken from the only home they've ever known. Hopefully, the children adapt well."

I threw that last bit over my shoulder as I swept past her, my head held high.

Just as the lady of the house should.

Chapter Nine

THE NEXT FEW weeks passed in a blur, so content Luc and I were. For the first few days after our wedding, Margaux and Jeanne had cared for the girls so Luc and I might have a measure of newlywed privacy in Luc's chambers. Twice did we hear screaming and the sounds of something fragile crashing, and Anne had rushed in to assure us everything was under control.

Luc had laughed in that deep rolling laugh at this.

"If Ella is involved, and I am certain she is, then nothing is under control."

And we laughed and laughed until we found ourselves under the covers again.

By the third day, we emerged and began the daunting task of blending his small family with mine. And to be honest, I had fretted over this.

Genevieve and Finette had not known their father long, but the time they did have with him had marked my girls, especially Genevieve, and she was cautious in welcoming Luc and his rough-and-tumble daughter. She hung back, her pale blue eyes watching life at Chateau Fournier unfold before she jumped into it. And from Ella's reaction to Genevieve, I didn't blame her.

No wonder Ella was lonely. Having been an only child for so long, the sole focus of her father, had created a bit of a spoiled brat. But then, weren't my own girls spoiled, having enjoyed the unending attentions of their mother? I had thought they might begrudge any time I spent, or tried to spend, with Ella. Instead, they encouraged it. I guess they too saw the sad little girl under the ash and dirt.

Finette, oh my chestnut haired *petite fille*, surprised me. She opened her arms to everyone at Chateau Fournier, Ella included. Every day, Finette gathered her dolls and toys, placed them in a fabric-covered box, and brought them to Ella's room. Some days, when Ella didn't permit the traumas of her youth to overwhelm her, she'd smile and open her door wide for Finette, play with her toys, even share her own. Those days, I often hovered just outside Ella's door frame and listened in on their childhood play. They giggled and cooed and shared their dolls and cradles and dishes like true sisters. Those days, I loved Ella more than ever, not because her behavior was divine, but because she was treating my baby girl like her very own sister — she was making this fantastic dream of our family real. And I loved her for that.

Other days, though, Finette's gesture to play was not received well at all. Those days, when Ella slammed the door on Finette or tried to take her toys away, Finette would flee and find me, climb up on my lap, and cry her heart out until she had no tears left. When I offered to speak to Ella, she flicked her eyes to me in horror.

"*Non*, Maman! She is so sad. She doesn't know the right thing to do when she's sad. She hasn't had a Maman to cuddle her when she's sad, and Monsieur Luc is kind to her, but he's gone with work a lot. So, he can't cuddle her when she needs it." Dear Finette wiped her tears from her plump cheeks. "I will just try again tomorrow."

Oh, my heart rented in two every time Finette said she would try again! Her heart was so open, and she was ready to be Ella's very close sister. Any mother would be fortunate in Finette.

She was even loving to Luc. She didn't hesitate to climb in his lap, hold his hand, or ask him for help. Finette was ready for a father, and tall, muscular Luc stepped into that role perfectly. I couldn't help but notice, however, that when she did this, Ella's eyes narrowed, and her face reddened to the collar of her dress. I wondered if that played into Ella's behavior, if she was reacting badly to Finette's offer of play on days when she was jealous of her father's attention to Finette.

After a few weeks of this dance, I pulled Jeanne aside and asked her for her counsel. After all, she and Margaux were with the girls most often and had the best perspective. One that was not tainted by childhood.

"Jeanne," I called out as she brought sheets to the girls' chambers. Finette and Genevieve shared a room — they wanted to be close — while Ella's quarters were a few more steps down the hall. "May I speak with you?"

She entered my quarters with a light bow. "Milady. Is something amiss? Did I do something wrong?" Jeanne fidgeted with the sheets with her eyes lowered. I patted her hand in reassurance.

"Oh, no, Jeanne. Not at all! I have a question about the girls, about Ella, if I might get your insight?"

Jeanne's face brightened, and she stood straighter. "*Oui*, Madame. What do you want to know?"

I picked at the embroidery on my sleeve. How to best frame this question?

"Have you noticed any changes with Ella? Maybe when she sees her father with Finette? Or Genevieve?"

It was a vague question, but I didn't want to plant any seeds.

"Changes? What do you mean? She still plays in the dirt and cinders and is a monster when it comes to bathtime."

"But not with either of the girls?"

Jeanne bit her lip. "I don't know Ella well enough, but I think she is sad and jealous. And if she sees either of the girls getting attention, she might act out. It is common with children to behave that way."

I dropped my sleeve. I hadn't known such a thing! Her behavior was common?

"So, you don't think we have anything to worry about with her? Or the girls?"

Jeanne shook her head. "*Non*, Madame. She will come around. Children are nothing if not adaptable."

Nodding at her sage words, I waved her off. She gathered the sheets against her chest and returned to the hall.

Maybe she was right. Maybe Ella's behavior was normal, and I shouldn't overreact.

Slowly, Genevieve warmed to Luc, but not to Ella as I had hoped. She was kind to Ella – Genevieve didn't have a mean bone to speak of – but she completed her schooling with Margaux, their governess, then spent the rest of her day reading, sewing, in the gardens, or following me around.

I knew Genevieve didn't care for Ella's dirty nature. Playing in cinders or dirt, wearing stained clothes, these things could bring Genevieve to a near faint, a trait Luc and I laughed over in the nighttime privacy of our chambers. Luc called her our "perfect princess."

One cloudy day, as autumn snaked its cool arms around the air and squeezed tight, Genevieve wandered into the gardens to find me digging up the rest of the potatoes.

"Maman, we have servants for that? What would papa Luc think to see your hand dirty?" She curled up her berry-pink lip. Oh, how dirt disgusted her! I smiled and held up my dirt-encrusted fingernails to her.

"True, *ma fille*, but he also knows I enjoy being in the gardens, finding solace in the feel of the earth on my fingers, in the smell of the plants, even in the bite of the cold. Plus, then I can do this!"

I lunged at her with my dirty hands curved into claws, and she screeched as she jumped back. I sat hard on my feet and laughed. After Genevieve recovered from her horrified fright, she giggled back.

"Oh, Maman, I don't know how you do that. Don't scare me like that again."

My hands resumed their word in the dirt. "I promise, *ma chou*. What are you doing with yourself today? Reading? Are you finished with your schoolwork with Madame Margaux?" I used my bent wrist to wipe a loose black strand of hair from my eyes. Several locks had loosed from my kerchief as I worked.

Genevieve didn't respond right away and stared off into the distance, past the wall, as though she could see all the way to the Palace House at Toulouse. I wiped my eyes again and peered at my daughter. Something was bothering her.

"Genevieve?" I prodded gently.

"Some days, I don't care for my schooling with Madame Margaux."

I sat up straight at this. Genevieve adored schooling, reading, even her numbers – a subject that had eluded me in my youth. She had never complained before.

"What do you mean? Do you not care for the material? Or is it the way Margaux presents it?"

She shrugged offhandedly, her brilliantly beautiful face stoic and emotionless.

"Often, it seems as though she cares only for what Ella is learning. Finette and I, well, we are left to our studies. I can help Finette, I rather enjoy doing that." A slight smile alighted her face, and my heart melted at that smile. She looked like an angel when she smiled.

Was another girl ever so beautiful as my Genevieve? And she was smart and kind, no wonder Ella was jealous. And I knew that the comparison of the two girls probably played into Margaux's protective nature. Ella was beautiful in her own right – a blonde-haired, blue-eyed cherub – but nothing like my Genevieve. Genevieve had the type of beauty that could well catch the eye of a royal, something Luc had intimated more than once. And he did have several connections to the palace, and a mother could dream largely for her daughter.

"Maybe Ella needs help. Not every girl is as clever as you are."

Genevieve sucked on her lip as she considered my words.

"That makes sense. I did not think of it that way. She does have trouble focusing on her work, and her reading is a bit slow, not much better than Finette's. I think I was being jealous."

I wiped my hands on the cloth by my knees. Once they were clean, I held my arms out to Genevieve, who slipped into them with familiar ease.

"Sometimes it can be difficult to see things from a different perspective if we are feeling hurt. And I know Ella can be a difficult child. So if Margaux needs to work with her, then we must accept that and be happy that someone is able to help her when she needs help."

Genevieve rested her head against my shoulder. "It seems more than that. Sometimes I feel like she is ignoring us or is angry if we have a question when she is working with Ella."

I ran my fingers through Guinevere's silky black tresses. "Remember that she is human, Ginny. She might be frustrated that Ella needs the additional assistance. Maybe you could offer to help Ella too, if the opportunity presents itself?"

It was asking a lot of my oldest daughter, but her kind nature won out.

"Maman, that's a good idea. I don't know if she will want my help, but school is easy for me. If I can help make it easier for Ella, or even for Madame Margaux in teaching us, then I will."

She ended her sentence with an earnest oomph, and my chest throbbed against her. Was a mother ever more proud of her daughter? Non, I don't believe so. How was I so blessed with such a marvelous family?

"That's my girl. And I will speak to Margaux, to see if we can come up with a solution to give Ella the attention she needs while still making sure you and Finette are receiving your schooling as well. How does that sound?"

Genevieve threw her slender arms around my neck.

"Oh, Maman. That sounds wonderful. *Merci*!"

After mercilessly scrubbing my hands until every last trace of dirt was gone, I adjusted my hair, pinning it back with a delicate gold filigree hair comb, and went in search of Margaux.

I only had Genevieve's side of the story to go on, and I wasn't about to accuse Margaux of inappropriate behavior, or Ella for that matter, until I heard both sides. The truth, I well knew, was somewhere in between.

Margaux was in the library, stacking books on a table. Her stout form was encased in a plain gray dress, and I had a horrible thought that she resembled a German sausage. Chastising myself for such a vitriolic thought toward a member of this house, I cleared my throat and smiled widely at her.

"*Bonjour,* Margaux. How do you fare today?"

Margaux flicked her gaze at me then turned her attention back to her books. Why did I have the sensation that she was dismissing me?

"I'm well, Madame. And how are you this day?"

Her voice was kind, so I probably misinterpreted her movements. "I'm well. How is schooling going with the girls? Having three can be a handful. Are you able to balance them?"

Margaux's hands froze and her gaze turned on me, hard and questioning.

"Are you suggesting that I'm not doing my job well?"

Mon Dieu! Was that how the question sounded?

I sat at one of the hardback chairs and lay my hand over my heart. "Oh, Margaux, forgive me! I was suggesting no such thing. I just want to make sure you have everything you need and that the girls are behaving for you." I tried to make sure my tone was light, inviting. It seemed to work. Margaux's hard face relaxed.

"Oh, of course. As a mother, you are interested in your children's education. Even Ella's."

My brow scrunched at her. "Of course, Ella. She is one of my daughters now. I am very concerned for her education, just as I am for Genevieve and Finette."

"But she's not your daughter. I wouldn't think you'd be as concerned."

I licked my lips and tamped down my rising temper. It would do no good to pick a fight with the governess.

"I don't know what you've seen in other households," I said slowly, keeping my tone level, "but in this house, they are all my daughters. They are all Luc's daughters. And if anything, I worry about Ella more, because she's seemed to struggle with my wedding to her father more than any of the children. I would hate for her to think that she's not as important, when she is very important to me. She may not be the daughter of my body, but she's the daughter of my heart because she's Luc's daughter. And that is the way we will think of her."

Margaux's stern gaze never wavered. Still, she nodded her head, accepting my declaration.

"Well, you are right. I've had to work with her because she's struggling and not paying attention. I've had to give her more hands on attention."

"And are Genevieve and Finette behaving for you, then? When you need to work with Ella?"

Margaux shrugged. "I don't quite know. Finette is an eager student, and she willingly works with Genevieve when I'm busy. Genevieve, however, seems to resent it when I work with Ella individually."

I had been right – both parties were viewing the situation through a viscous slant.

"I know that Genevieve is clever, and school comes easy to her. She doesn't mind helping Finette. But she can also grow bored if not challenged. We need to make sure she has enough to keep her busy. Perchance she might help Ella at times, relieving you to work with Finette? That might be a good challenge for her." I couldn't stop the smile that came from that idea. Perhaps it might help Ella and Genevieve grow closer as sisters should be.

"*Non!*" Margaux barked out, and I jumped at her outburst. "No, I will help Ella. I'll just give Genevieve more work if she is not challenged."

I didn't want to believe that her voice was hostile, as though she didn't care for the idea of working with Genevieve at all, but I pushed it to the side. Most likely, Margaux felt threatened, that I was yet suggesting she couldn't do her job well.

"I will speak to Monsieur Fournier. Perchance we should hire another governess for Genevieve. Since she is older, a separate governess might work better. That would permit you time to focus on the younger girls."

Margaux's lip twitched, but when she spoke, her voice was calm.

"If you think that to be best, Madame," she answered before picking up her papers and leaving me alone in the library.

It hadn't been the best encounter, to be sure. However, a solution had presented itself, one that I needed to mention to Luc that evening.

In addition to discussing another governess with Luc, which he readily agreed to, a second topic arose.

"What do you think of these rooms?" he asked me suddenly. He sat by the fire and I on his lap. His eyes caught the reflection of the flames in the hearth, dancing both with the orange light and with joy at having me close to him.

That needs to be near to me was a desire I had noticed right away. If he wasn't working, he preferred that I be by his side, touching him, holding his hand, sitting on his lap, kissing him. Over and over, he told me he needed to touch me, that his life was gray unless his hands were on me, and that if work permitted it, he would take me with him every day.

I sighed every time he said those romantic words. Luc had so much love to share, and he wanted to share it with me. Had such a loving man ever existed before now? I could not imagine. My breath caught when he touched me, and I thanked God every day that he led me to this man.

"What do you mean? They are fine quarters."

He glanced around, his strong chin pointing at the rafters.

"I don't know about that. Don't you think they are rather, well, staid? Bland?"

My eyes followed his glance. True, most of the quarters were wood, darker shades, and the rug on the floor was plain gray and matched the gray curtains hanging in the windows.

"I have light and color in my life now that I have you. Shouldn't the rooms we share reflect that?"

His eyes returned to mine, and I shuddered at the intensity of his gaze. He leaned in to nuzzle my neck, and the rich scents of his bath and his musk made my head spin. I gave a sultry laugh and pushed him back to study the rooms.

Luc was correct, as usual. The rooms were rather bland, rather gray, an eternally rainy day. And our life together was sunshine and butterflies and joy. Our rooms should reflect that.

"They are fairly drab. Should we change that?"

"*Oui*! Whatever you like. Tell me and I will hire builders and mason and seamstresses, and we will craft a room that is bright and beautiful, like you."

"Like me?" I squealed. His grin widened.

"Almost like you. There is nothing on this earth as beautiful as you."

Then he kissed me, and that was the end of our conversation.

Chapter Ten

A SLENDER WOMAN named Joan and her husband, Jacques, arrived early the next morning, their arms laden with drawings and swatches in a rainbow invasion.

Jacques didn't speak much — he didn't have to. Joan didn't stop talking. From the moment she entered the main hall, she bubbled with a champagne bottle of words that popped and wouldn't stop flowing.

"It is so nice to meet the new Madame of the house! Are you loving it here? I can only imagine,

"We should see some wonderful changes by the end of the week. Once it's done, we'll have a grand tour, as if we are touring the royal palace itself. What do you think?"

The girls cheered, and I kissed their cheeks before they slid off the bed and raced for their rooms. Jeanne would be waiting for them for baths and bedtime.

As they left, I noticed a pair of hesitant eyes at the edge of the door frame.

"Ella?" I said softly. "Do you want to come in and see what's going on?"

I reached out my hand to her. She entered the room on wary toes but didn't take my hand. She stood in the center of the room, her head moving this way and that, trying to see everything at once.

"Why are you changing it?" she asked.

"Your father thought that, since we are so happy as a family, that our rooms should be as cheery as we are. There's too much gray in here, don't you think?"

"My mother liked the gray," Ella said in a tight tone. My heart sunk to my feet. This was not the turn I had hoped for.

"I understand that. And gray is a fine color. But your father wants to start fresh. Too many memories can make us sad. We should hold on to our memories, but it's not healthy to live in them. We have this amazing life ahead of us, and we should celebrate in it. Changing the room, it's a part of that celebration."

Ella's fair head circled the room again.

"Well, I don't like it." Her words were a proclamation,

"Ella! You should watch your tone. Be respectful of your elders," I lectured her, hoping to make an impact.

It didn't have the effect I intended. Before I could say anything more, she stormed off with a scowl.

My heart sunk to the pit of my stomach. What was I doing wrong? I just wanted her to be happy, as happy as my girls and I were. As happy as Luc was. Couldn't she be happy for him, her own father? Hot tears of sadness and defeat, burned under my eyelids. I heard the floorboards squeak and wiped at my eyes. Only Luc had enough weight to make that board protest, and I wiped my face with the back of my hand.

I wasn't quick enough.

"*Mon amour! Mon Coeur!* Why do you weep?"

Luc raced to my side and held my face between his warm palms. I melted into his touch.

"I've tried everything, Luc, yet Ella still despises me. She was just here and told me she doesn't like the room. I've asked her to keep her dresses clean, and the more I ask, the dirtier she gets. She's still mean to Finette at times, but with me, it's all the time. I don't know what else to do. All I want is for our house to be full of love, of the love we share. But Ella hates me, and I feel so guilty."

This time the tears fell freely, and Luc, my gentle, loving Luc, kissed the tears away.

"Oh, Corrine. You're doing nothing wrong. I've seen how patient you are with Ella, more patient than I have been. You're an amazing mother, even to this angry little girl, and it makes me love you even more. The more spiteful she is, the more your try to love her, and that tells me I have found the most perfect wife I could. She will come around. One day she will see you as her mother, and you will have that house full of love that you so desire and deserve."

And as he held me in that torn apart room, as torn apart as I felt, I believed him.

Chapter Eleven

ONCE THE ROOM was completed, I struggled to keep the girls out. Their favorite was to play with their dolls on the new salon furniture, the light fabric imprinted with leaves, a warm compliment to the walls and the rug. The whole room seemed luminescent in the day, as if the brighter fabrics caught the light and held it in the room. When the girls played on the new, larger settee, they glowed like stars, and their girlish giggling was music to my ears. Even Genevieve joined them a few times, though she claimed to be too old to play with dolls.

One late autumn day, when the light was so pale it struggled to push past the cloud and the cold wind found every gap and crevice, whistling its icy song, Finette left the settee, her play complete and her dolls went with her. Ella, however, remained on the settee. Her gaze focused on a random point outside the window. Anne had brought up my clothing from the laundry, and I had told her I'd put it away in the newly retouched wardrobe. My eyes kept glancing around the room, disbelief that I might have a room so fine it was fit for a princess.

I was silent as I placed my chemises and underskirts in their places. I didn't want to break this calm silence with Ella. It was the first time she'd remained in my presence without anger.

"What are those?" Her tiny voice broke the silence. I glanced over at her.

That focused gaze had shifted from the window to the high self of the wardrobe. A slow smile spread across my face. I knew exactly what she was looking at. Reaching high, I grasped the glass slippers and brought them out.

I sat on the bed and patted the quilted blanket next to me. She scrambled over and climbed up. She didn't touch me when she sat, but this was the closest she'd ever been. I handed a shoe to her.

"These are glass slippers. Have you ever seen such a thing?"

She turned the shoe over in her hand, letting it catch what little light penetrated the cut glass windows. It still sparkled as it had on my wedding day.

"I wore them on the day I married your father. One day, when you get married, I will let you wear them, too."

She looked up at me, her blue eyes wide and, for once, soft. I could see the pretty little girl under the angry mask and my heart wept for her. I wanted to put my arm around her, pull her close, smell her hair and make her feel loved. I didn't. Ella reminded me of a deer, and if I moved, I'd startle her and she'd run away, I was certain.

"How did you walk in these? Was it hard?"

"Not too hard," I answered, holding the other one before me. Ella's eyes moved from one to the other.

"Where did you get these?"

"Your father had them made for me. What a generous gift, *oui*?"

Ella's hand clasped the shoe tightly, and for a moment I thought she'd run away with the right shoe. She turned it around in her hand once more, then that angry mask shadowed her face again. Before I could react, reach out and take back the shoe, she threw the glass slipper across the room. My chest stopped as I watched it arc in the air, and the air rushed from my lungs when it hit the run. It slid to the edge and made a light tinkling sound as it hit the wooden floor. I raced after it, yelling.

"Ella! What were you thinking? Your father paid hard earned coin for these shoes!"

She flung herself off the bed and raced out of the room as Luc entered. He'd heard the commotion and found me crouched at the edge of the rug, cradling the precious shoe in my arms.

"What is it? What's happened?" His face was pale, his eyes round. I'd caused him to panic with my screams. Why had I done that? I know better than to cause a panic where there is none.

"My apologies, Luc. I was showing the glass slippers to Ella. We were having a good moment, then she thew one across the room. I thought it was unblemished because it landed on the rug, but it chipped when it struck the floor. I'm so sorry for yelling. It was not worth yelling over."

Luc took my hand in a gentle grip and helped me rise. "Let me see the shoe," he asked.

I handed it over and he peered at the damage. It was truly just a small chip.

"I can see if the glass blower or the cobbler can fix this." He set the shoe on the small table by the door, then took both of my hands in his. "And it is yelling over. *Oui*, it's just a shoe, but it was a gift from me to you, and you were generous to let Ella hold it. I will talk to her, reprimand her. She's taken this behavior too far, and it's time it was dealt with."

I didn't realize I'd been holding my breath until I released it in a rush. Though I hadn't known it, part of me had been hoping Luc would take a stronger hand with his daughter, and this had been the final straw for him. I also hoped that a stern reprimand from her father might set Ella on a better path in our home. Truthfully, I was tired of being the one who had to be patient, who had to deal with her angry outbursts all the time.

"I think she needs that. Children need discipline. It's a way to show love. And the sooner she realizes how she should behave, the happier everyone in the home will be."

Luc's clear forehead crinkled. "Has she been that bad? I've been working so much. I haven't been here. And I know you would gloss over everything so as not to worry me. Maybe I've been too absent. Tell me, Corrine, how bad has it been?"'

"It's gotten a lot better as of late," I told him a half-truth. "She's been wonderful for Margaux. She and Finette play together often. Even Genevieve has joined in. She's still a dirty mess much of the time, but that's not a real issue. Her anger, what she still has of it, she directs at me, but I can handle it. I'm a grown woman with the support of her husband and daughters. I can be as patient as I need to be for her. For you."

Luc shook his head, his tawny locks falling against his forehead. I had to suppress the desire to sweep it away. Now was not the time to distract him.

"*Non*, you've been patient enough. I will have a talk with her and deal her punishment on the morn."

He pulled me close, and I rested my head against his chest. His heart spoke to me in the steady cadence of his heartbeat, telling me that he'd always take care of me. His strong, steady heartbeat, the swan song of my life. I smiled against his shirt. Taking a firmer hand with Ella was the first step into fully achieving the family we desired.

I underestimated Luc, and as much as I loved him, I feared he might have taken the wrong approach with Ella when he decided to punish her.

He didn't do anything that night — our anger at her behavior was too raw — and he worried he wouldn't behave the way a good father should. I embraced him that night in our beautiful new bedding and assured him he was the best of fathers, but I also agreed that it might be better to let our ire and irritation cool and speak with Ella in the morn, when we had calmer heads.

Breakfast the following morning was a quiet affair, with the random tinkling of silverware the lone sound breaking the somber mood. Genevieve and Finette must have sensed something wasn't right, even if they didn't know what had happened with Ella, because they were as quiet as church mice. They spooned their porridge into their mouths in silent movements — their spoons clicked soundlessly against their bowls.

Ella didn't eat. She sat at her blue porcelain bowl and glared at it, as she glared at everything, her arms crossed over her slender chest in protest. Luc flicked his soft ocean blue eyes at me and took my hand before addressing Ella.

"Do you have anything to say about what happened yesterday, Ella?" Luc asked in a tempered tone. Not angry, not accusing, but with enough force to compel her to respond.

Ella didn't look at her father, but those rosy lips puckered more. Oh, but she was a headstrong one! Genevieve and Finette's eyes went wide as they sat back to watch the breakfast events unfold.

"Ella?" Luc asked, his tone gentle, prodding.

"You never bought Maman glass shoes."

My breath turned to ice in my chest. She was upset over the fact Luc bought me the shoes? Try as I might, I had the sense I would never understand what was going on in Ella's little blonde head. I don't think anyone did.

Luc squeezed my hand and leaned forward, closer to Ella. "You don't really know what I did or didn't buy her. You weren't born until a year after we married, and she died before she could show you items like that. And you are right, I didn't buy her glass shoes, because I didn't know such a thing

141

existed until just this spring. However, I did buy her other things for our wedding, including a special dress, and I still have that put up so you might wear it one day, when you wed."

Ella's eyes glimmered with tears, and though I still harbored a bit of ire at her, my heart wrenched. She was a lost little girl, after all.

"You still have Maman's dress?" Her voice sounded hopeful. It was the sweetest I'd ever heard her speak.

"Of course. And it was kind of your new mother to offer her shoes to go with it. You should have thanked her instead of trying to destroy the shoes."

His tone took on a slight tone of displeasure, and from the corner of my eye, I caught Genevieve and Finette exchange shocked expressions. So they hadn't known. Thankfully, they remained silent.

"She's not my mother," Ella spat out, her eyes turning from sweet to ice chips as she flicked her gaze from her father to me.

"Well, that is a discussion for another day. Regardless, she made a wonderful offer to you, and you treated it and her shabbily. I think you owe Corrine an apology."

Ella's arms squeezed tight over her chest, again in her silent protest.

"Ella, will you apologize to Corinne?"

From the cutting look on her face, I should have expected what happened next. But I really couldn't believe she'd do it.

She glared at her father, then lifted a hand, slow and steady, and before any of us could react, she slammed her hand into her delicate bowl and sent it flying right at me. It tipped over at the edge of the table and right onto my lap with an audible plop.

"Maman!" Genevieve screeched, reaching for me.

"Ella!" Luc thundered, pounding his fist onto the table, making the serving ware rattle. "You will go to your room until I say you can come out!"

"Non! You can't make me!" She screamed and jumped from her chair, ready to run out the door.

She smacked into Margaux, who appeared at the doorway like a specter.

"Ella, *mademoiselle*! What is this?" The squat woman bent and wiped Ella's cheeks with her thumb. A wave of irritation washed over me. Ella was fine. No one had thrown food at *her*.

"Madame Renaud, leave her," Luc commanded. "She is to be punished. No rolling in the dirt or cinders for her. She is to take to her room, and if she doesn't apologize to Corrine today, she will be there tomorrow, complete with a list of chores. She will learn to appreciate all that she has!"

Margaux paled — evidently Luc was the one person in the house she did fear — but as she turned, I thought I saw her lips twitch, almost in disdain. Then Jeanne was at my side with a cloth, helping Genevieve clean my skirts. It was no use — I was going to have to change and have this rich aubergine gown laundered. As long as they got most of it off so I could ascend the steps without drizzling porridge on the rugs, that would suffice.

Luc returned his attentions to the table.

"I am so sorry, *mon amour*. I can't believe she did that. It's been years since her mother passed, and months since you've joined our household. She must learn to accept her life as it is. Otherwise, she will be angry and continue to blame everything on you for the rest of her days."

I patted his strong arm. "We just need to give her time." I wanted to be on Luc's side, but I also felt compelled to be on Ella's side, the poor sad thing.

"*Non*," he protested, kissing my cheek. "And I have a mind to dismiss Madame Renaud. She caters too much to Ella's sour behavior, I think."

A flush covered my chest and face. That was an idea I agreed with, but at the same time, I worried that if Margaux left, Ella would feel she lost the only person who still cared for her, a fairy godmother we forced away, and I told Luc this.

"I believe rather we should encourage Margaux to help her accept her lot, help her realize that she has such wonder in her life and to focus on that. I fear that if we dismiss the governess, it will just be something else that Ella will react against."

Luc nodded, his clenched jaw relaxing. "I will defer to your greater wisdom, *ma femme*. It seems you are in good hands. I have to meet up with several merchants today. I shall be home for supper."

He lifted my hand, the noble man he was, and kissed it, then winked at the girls and departed the dining room.

"Ignore her, Maman," Genevieve told me, sounding so mature for her age. "Let's go upstairs and get you cleaned up."

Jeanne waved us on and started to clear the breakfast dishes as my beloved daughters ushered me upstairs. I kissed the top of their heads as we walked — if only Ella could behave as agreeably as they did.

Chapter Twelve

ELLA SPENT TWO days in her room, but after the second day, finished with chores that she pouted over, she came to our room after Luc had changed into his lounging robe. She dropped her head, and said "I'm sorry," in a barely audible voice.

Luc opened his mouth to speak, but I didn't want anything to ruin this moment. I placed a hand on his upper arm, then lifted my skirts to crouch low to Ella. While she kept her eyes on the floor and her body stiff, I still hugged her.

"Thank you for that, Ella." I cupped the back of her head, where her soft golden curls settled against her neck. "I know this is hard. It's not what you expected. But I do care for you, I love you, and I want you to be able to move past your sadness and enjoy this family we have. I will be here for you always."

She didn't answer and withdrew from my embrace, dragging her feet as she left. Luc reached for me and took both my hands in his.

"I love you, Corinne. I love how you care for me, care for Ella, care for our family. No other woman would be as patient as you are with Ella. Or as patient with me, and I love you for that."

He hugged me tight, running his hands over my length of hair flowing down my back. I shivered as his fingers caressed my neck with each brush of my hair.

My heart surged at Ella's apology, at Luc's words, and the pure magic of this brisk, late fall night. I couldn't imagine myself happier than I was at that moment.

Late that night, Luc had settled by the fire with his lounging robe, and I had hung up my heavy brocade gown. Anne was brushing it out when a tentative knock came at our ornate wooden door.

"*Entrez*," Luc announced his is rumbling tone.

Jeanne walked in, her head low and a small dress in her hands.

"*Monsieur*, *Madame*, I have a small issue I need to bring to your attention."

At first, a flare of worry pulsed through me, but then she lifted the gown. It was worn, sagging, had a small stain on the hem, and seemed far too small for any of our girls.

"Genevieve and Finette, they have outgrown their gowns. The summer fruit and fresh air did its job well. I checked to see if Genevieve or Ella had gowns that might fit Finette to pass them down. Genevieve had few dresses at all, and most were in the same shape. Ella has several dresses, but they are mostly stained or torn, and Finette would only be able to wear them for a short time at best."

Luc turned his serene blue gaze to me. "Corinne, do the girls not have dresses?"

I bit my lip and dropped my gaze to my toes peeping from under my embroidered shift. The girls had a couple of frocks made when Luc and I wed, but not many, and that had been months ago. I had noticed Genevieve wearing her nicer dress most days, as her play dress didn't fit, but with Luc's generosity over the past months, I hesitated to ask him for more. And if Genevieve and Finette were to have new gowns, I wanted Ella to have them, too. I'd made so much progress with her, I despised the thought that she might feel left out if we didn't buy her a new garment as well.

Luc didn't wait for my answer — it was obvious from my stance.

"Jeanne, we will have the seamstress come tomorrow for the girls, and I will order fabric to arrive as well. They will have several fine, new gowns made for fall and winter."

"Ella, too," I added. "A dress or two for her."

"Non." Luc's voice wasn't severe, but forceful. "She doesn't care for the gowns she presently has. I'll not have gowns made when all she does is roll around in the dirt or hearth ashes. She can wear what she has until she outgrows them."

"Luc, I fear she will feel left out. We've come so far . . ."

He nodded at me. "I will speak to her and tell her it's my decision and why. She will understand. Thank you for bringing this up to us, Jeanne," he said to the maid, dismissing her.

Jeanne smiled, curtsied, and left. Anne had finished her work, and I dismissed her as well.

Luc swirled his brandy in his round glass and watched me flit around the room.

"You're worried about these gowns, about Ella," he said, holding his hand out to me.

I grasped it, and he pulled me onto his lap. The heat of the dancing flames warmed my back, and the soft crush of his velvet robe cushioned my face where I rested it on his shoulder.

"I just don't want her to feel left out. You are too generous with us."

Luc wrapped his strong arm around my waist, and I snuggled closer. He kissed the top of my head.

"She won't. She's had life handed her to her on a silver platter. She will understand. And, *mon amour*, I cannot be generous enough. I would give you my life if you asked for it."

I rubbed my hand on his chest.

"I have your heart. It's all I need."

The seamstress arrived the next day with her assistant and heaping piles of fabric unlike anything I'd ever seen in my life. Genevieve and Finette stood at the edge of the main hall with matching, wide-eyed expressions of surprise.

"For us?" Finette kept asking. I reached over the fabric and kissed the top of her head.

"Oui, for you," Luc told her.

Genevieve's tentative hand caressed the top bolt of fabric, a pale blue and yellow lawn. She was speechless, but the joy on her face was unmistakable, and I laid my hand on my chest and glanced over at my love. He tipped his head, a slight smile tugging at his lips. Oh, this man was sent from my very dreams.

"What are you doing?" a slight voice called from the hall. I spun to see Ella in the archway.

"Genevieve and Finette need new dresses, so I called Madame Louis in," Luc said.

He raised an eyebrow at Ella, as if waiting for her to confront him. Luc didn't have to wait long.

"Why didn't you call me? Don't I get new dresses?"

"What happened to the dresses you got this summer?"

Genevieve stepped away from the fabric and tried to hide behind my skirts. She was weary of Ella's tantrums. Finette, however, watched with interest.

Ella's lips thinned. "They are getting too small. I need new ones."

Luc laughed lightly, then turned to me, his gaze intense. "I shall be home tonight."

"And I shall be waiting for you," I promised.

I heard Luc in the hall late after dinner. The house was quiet, and I was dressed in my shift, awaiting him in our bedroom. Another voice, Ella's, carried through the walls, and I went to the door, opening it a bare inch to see what was going on.

Ella's thin body was clad in her stained nightshirt. Jeanne had put her to bed, but she obviously hadn't gone to sleep, instead waiting for her father's return. Her tiny face twisted with angst.

"Why didn't you get me any dresses?" she spat out.

Luc knelt in front of her and put his arm around her shoulders.

"Ella, please. They needed the dresses, and you didn't. Don't you think you're being rather selfish?"

She didn't respond, but her bottom lip protruded farther. She despised her father's explanation.

"I don't want them here. Why did you bring them here? It was fine without them. Make them leave."

I felt that I was choking. Here I was thinking I'd made progress with this little girl, and now she was telling her father she wanted us gone. I leaned against the cool wall, pressing my forehead to my hand. What was I to do? Would we ever be the family I wanted for Luc and myself? Why was it always Ella causing our problems? For the first time since I'd met the girl, my heart turned to stone. How dare she make her father's life so complicated? I wasn't angry at her vitriol toward me, but at how much this must be hurting my beloved.

"You have to understand that Corinne and her daughters are part of our family now," Luc continued in his tender voice. I marveled that he could keep this voice level and blinked back the fiery tears that burned in my eyes. "I love you, Ella. But I also love Corinne and her daughters. We are a family now. She is your mother —"

"Stepmother," Ella spat at her father.

"And her daughters are your sisters," he continued, as if she hadn't spoken. "You must accept it. We want to have a full, happy family. It's time for you to put your sadness and your anger behind you and become part of this family. Corinne is your mother now and you must accept it."

She stomped her foot. *"Non,"* she protested.

"If you love me, Ella, then you will accept it. To do otherwise will break my heart."

I squinted into the hall, waiting to see what Ella's reaction would be. The girl didn't hug her father back, but she didn't pull away either. Maybe that was progress? Luc kissed her clear forehead.

"Now, go to bed, and tomorrow we shall start anew and be one happy family."

Dropping her head so her curls hid her petulant face, she moped down the dimly lit hallway to her room.

Luc stood, and I scrambled away from the door to the chair by the flickering warm hearth and retrieved my book. By the time he opened the door and entered, I appeared unaware that anything had transpired with Ella. He unbuttoned his woolen coat, and I went to him, taking his coat from his hands and placing it on its hook. Luc rubbed his hand over his chest before removing his flaxen shirt.

"I spoke to Ella," he said, breaking the silence.

"About what?" I asked in completely feigned ignorance.

"She is still unhappy. I told her she needed to get past it and start enjoying the happiness that our family can bring. That it would make my heart happy if she did so."

I helped him strip his shirt off as I considered his words. Such a diplomat, he was. He rubbed his chest again. I placed my hand atop his. How she must have pained his heart.

"I am certain your request made an impact on Ella. She is sure to behave appropriately and find her happiness with us."

But as I hung up his shirt, I wondered. Ella had not looked happy when she left his embrace and went to bed.

Chapter Thirteen

MADAME LOUIS RETURNED a few days later, her arms laden with a rainbow of colors, frills, crinoline, and ruffles. Genevieve and Finette thundered down the stairs when I called for them. Before Luc could make it out of our bedroom, the girls were in the main hall, ready to claim their gowns.

Finette held a divine, high-waisted lilac gown to her shoulders, the purple ribbon at the waist fluttering against the ground.

"May I try it on, Maman? I'm in my shift as it is!" She danced to her question. Madame Louis handed a dress and accoutrements to Genevieve as I looked Finette over. She had no propriety, dressed in her thin shift as she was, but I couldn't deny her.

"Oui, try it on over your shift," I told her as I waved my hand in her direction.

With a quick flick of her arms, the gown was over her head and down her body, and she smoothed the skirts against her legs. The rounded short sleeves puffed up perfectly, and she spun around, watching the purple swirl at her feet. I grasped her shoulder and turned her back to me so I might tie the bow, lest she step on the end and rip it off the dress before she even wore it.

She looked like a porcelain doll, even with her mussed brown hair a nest on her head. And she looked beautiful.

"Luc!" I called up the stairwell. "Please come and see what your generosity has wrought!"

A creak sounded on the stairs and I flicked my eyes over, expecting to see Luc. Instead, Ella stepped into the main hall.

"Oh, Ella. Look at the dresses." I reached my hand to cup the curls at the base of her head. "I promise, next time, you'll get dresses, too. It's just you have so much, and Genevieve and Finette have so little, especially with winter coming."

Ella pointed at spinning Finette. "That doesn't look like a winter dress," she said in her flat, unexcited voice.

"It's probably for special events. I'm sure the other dresses are cold-weather dresses."

Keeping a sharp eye on Finette, Ella moved closer to her, and when one of Finette's ribbons flitted past Ella, she grabbed at it. She held tight, and Finette kept spinning.

The ripping sound was loud enough to bring everyone to a halt.

Finette finished her spin and stared at the strip of shimmery lilac fabric crumpled Ella's hand. Without saying a word, Finette burst into a spasm of tears.

"Finette, Finette, it's nothing," I told her, brushing past Ella to console her. "It was an accident!"

I knelt next to her and wiped at her cheeks. Finette lifted an accusatory finger at Ella.

"Non, Maman! She did it on purpose!"

Ella came over to Finette, holding out the ribbon. I thought she wanted to return it in an apologist if gesture. Then she threw it at Finette and, before I could move, she slapped Finette across the face. A red hand imprint inflamed Finette's cheek and her crying became screaming.

"Ella!" Luc's voice thundered across the room, and we turned to him. His shirt was undone, his chest peeking out from the creamy fabric. One arm rested against the wall as he leaned in the archway to the stairwell. How long had he been there? How much had he seen? "What is wrong with you?"

"I hate them, Father! I hate them all!"

"Ella!" he growled again, rubbing his bare chest. "What did I tell you last night?"

Luc's face was pale, and I had a sudden worry for him. Was Ella's behavior too much? Had he reached his tipping point?

"I don't care, Father!" she screeched and raced to the stairs where her father stood. "I hate them all and I want them gone!"

She stomped her bare foot on the ground, punctuating her anger. Margaux must have heard the commotion from the library as she entered the salon and went directly to Ella. Of course, she would.

I left the sobbing Finette to Madame Louis's skilled hands and moved to Luc.

"*Mon amour,* you don't look well. Please sit down." I took his hand to lead him to the overstuffed chair by the wall.

"Father!" Ella screamed again.

Luc's shoulders curved inward, and he shifted those cerulean eyes to me.

"Corinne. I'm sorry. I love you —"

Then he collapsed to the ground at my feet.

Ella screamed impossibly louder, but I didn't really hear her. Everything fell away as I crouched over Luc, rubbing at his back and arms, trying to wake him.

But he wouldn't wake, never again wake. I knew that as I shook him and called to him and begged him to stay by my side.

His hand clutched mine, but that was all. I knew he wasn't clutching it because he wanted to show he loved me or assure me.

He was clutching me hand in a death grip.

My Luc, my beloved, was dead.

I think I was screaming, too. If not aloud, then on the inside. My girls rushed to my side, covering me with their hands and hair, trying to console me, but I was inconsolable.

My love, my heart, my dream, everything bright and beautiful in this world that Luc gave me was dead with the man at my feet.

Someone had sent the footman to town and retrieved the doctor with our fastest horses. When he arrived, I had to be dragged away by Jeanne and Madame Louise. They sat me in the chair I had been trying to move for Luc, and we watched in sobbing misery as the doctor rolled Luc over and listened to his chest, checked his neck and face, then turned his sad, black eyes to me.

"I'm sorry, Madame Fournier. Seigneur Fournier is dead."

Then my world went black.

Chapter Fourteen

WE BURIED MY beloved husband in the Fournier cemetery at the far end of the Chateau Fournier gardens. The snow whipped around, but I felt nothing, no cold, no wind, nothing. My daughters' hands clasped mine, and they clung to me, even more than they had when Andre had died, but I didn't register it.

All I saw was gray. Dead leaves, dead grass, dead gardens, dead husband. Why? Why had the dream of my heart been destroyed before I had the chance to live in it fully with the man whom I loved and adored? Not even a year. We hadn't even had a year of bliss when he was taken from me.

I flicked my eyes across the snow-blurred air to the blonde girl standing in a gray woolen coat next to Margaux. I didn't want to blame her, I didn't. *I'm so sorry I couldn't win her love for you, mon amour,* I said in a prayer to Luc.

In my head, I knew it wasn't Ella's fault that her father had died, yet my heart . . . My heart didn't know the difference. My chest ached and turned to stone whenever I looked at the girl.

Her eyes were downcast and reddened ever since Luc had died. I'm sure his words in the hall, the words Ella didn't know I had heard, rang in her ears just as they rang in mine. Some of his final words to her.

Did Ella break his heart?

As much as I was loath to admit it, I think in some way, she did.

Then the funeral was over, and Anne took me up to our quarters, my quarters now. I was in a daze. I thanked God that at least Jeanne and Anne were there to watch over the girls — heavens knew I wasn't in any place to do so.

And Margaux was there for Ella. Everybody had somebody.

Except me. I had Luc, ocean-eyed, lion-haired, dimpled Luc, but not anymore.

I didn't bother to change. I remained in my mourning clothes.

I tried to sleep. I tried to close my eyes and let the miserableness of this day fall into oblivion, but I couldn't. My mind couldn't stop recalling every minute I had with Luc – his words, the timber of his voice, the feel of his hands on my hair, my back . . .

What was I going to do now?

A glimmer from inside my wardrobe kept catching my eyes. All my beautiful, colorful dresses of ruby, emerald, hyacinth, and scarlet. What use were those gowns now? Who would see me in them and compliment my dark beauty set against the rich fabrics? Not Luc.

I shoved them to the side, not caring if they wrinkled or tore. What use were these gowns to me now? I hated that they reminded me of everything I'd lost. Never again would I wear bright colors. My world was a dismal, steel gray, and my dress must reflect that. I pulled out my high-necked gray dress with the black-painted bone buttons. It was severe, and I never wore it with Luc. It was perfect for the next day, as I had no Luc memories with it.

My wedding gown and those glass shoes, I'd have to figure out what to do with those later. Perchance Anne might pack them away and store them in the high-roofed attic. That would be a fair sight better than having to see those cursed, everyday reminders of my short love with Luc.

I was exhausted, beyond exhausted, and when the early darkness crept through the windows, I slammed the curtains shut. A knock sounded at the door — I knew it would be Anne with a platter of food and encouraging words. I hadn't eaten since Luc died, and every day she brought food and a measure of comfort.

I didn't want either.

"Madame? I've brought a light dinner, soup and bread. Please eat," she begged, setting the platter on the table next to the other, untouched platter from the day before. "You must eat."

"How are the girls?" I asked. It had become my standard question.

"Genevieve and Finette are keeping to their room. They are lost without you."

As I am without Luc, I thought bitterly.

"And Ella had found a measure of comfort with Margaux," Anne continued.

"Of course she has," I said in a low voice.

"Pardon?"

"Nothing, Anne," I said louder, waving her off.

She took the day-old platter and left me to my sadness.

The next morning dawned just as gray as the previous days, as gray as all the days to come. I finally left my quarters, wearing my dark gray dress, and my black hair pulled back. A streak of white had formed, the stress of the loss of my beloved. I noticed it that morning as I sat at my vanity and put my hair in a thick bun. Aged — Luc's death had aged me.

I called out to the girls, and my two arrived in the hall. We made our way to the library where I expected to find Ella, but only Margaux was there, a sickeningly satisfied look on her sour mouth. I detested her and wanted to dismiss her. But then I'd have to deal with Ella on my own, and right now, I couldn't stand to be in the same room as her. Margaux remained in the house by the sheer virtue of my dislike for Luc's selfish daughter.

"I expected Ella to be here," I told her in a hard voice, one I never had before. Ugh, that word. Now my life was measured in tarnished spoons of before Luc's death and after Luc's death. "I'd like to speak to all the girls about how the house must now run."

Genevieve and Finette's teary eyes gazed up at me. Margaux, however, never even glanced my way.

"I don't think Ella will go along with anything you say, as she will never forgive you for the death of her father."

I placed a hand on my chest. "Did she say that to you? Well, there is much you don't know, Madame Renaud. Primarily, that Luc asked her the night before to be kind and accept her role in our family, because to do otherwise would pain his heart. Yet she still couldn't find it in her to behave, to accept us as her family. This lot? Her father's death? That, Madame Renaud, can only be blamed on Ella herself. Not on me as her mother."

The girls gasped as I spoke this harsh truth I'd hidden for days. Margaux didn't even flinch. She must have already known, and that knowledge tasted like ash in my dry mouth. Her hard face continued to stare at me, as though I was the cause of Ella's, and thus her own, misery.

"Regardless, Madame Fournier," Margaux said with her own added inflection that I didn't care to hear, "to Ella, you are nothing more than an evil stepmother who killed her father."

I raised my chin to the shorter, stout woman and drew myself up to my full, impressive height. My level of disdain for both her and Ella had reached its highest point.

"If that is her decision, so be it. I will accept my lot as stepmother." My voice held a sharp edge, harder than it ever had been in the whole of my life, and Margaux recoiled against the wall.

I knew I was more than the misnomer of evil stepmother, but neither Ella nor Margaux would believe anything else. And in my sadness and anger, I didn't care anymore. I had done everything right, with no avail. Thus, I would wear that title with pride, and with my silent apologies to Luc that I wasn't able to win the love of his daughter, I vowed to make sure Ella knew me as an evil stepmother, as wicked as she believed me to be. Maybe one day, if her behavior changed, she might win me, and my daughters, back.

I left the library, slamming the door behind me, then sent the remains of my heart, Genevieve and Finette, to their rooms. They were the only loves I had left in this world, and I vowed to shower them with all the adoration I hadn't been able to share with Luc. I would protect them and ensure their happiness in the future.

They were all I had left.

Then I descended the stairs, austere in dress and hair, hardened, and ready to assume my new role as the widowed, Madame of Chateau Fournier.

The End

Excerpt from Before the Magic Mirror

I CUT MY EYES to Werner, hoping he saw my silvery blue gaze. One smile from him was all I needed to make it through this soirée.

My mother had gone overboard with the engagement party, inviting the creme de la creme of our demesne. Everyone from neighboring barons to our solicitor, Hans Von Ruchse, attended, showering Werner and me with gifts. Werner's birthright as the future Prince-Bishop, the king of our canton, did matter when it came to gift giving. My favorite engagement gift was a bathing set with embroidered towels meant for Werner and I to bathe together. I had flushed with abashed warmth as I opened the velvet cloth bag to expose the exquisite set, as its use was obvious, but it only made my excitement about my upcoming nuptials grow.

My father was a lowly baron, but he was a wealthy one, and the king's coffers couldn't pass up the rich dowry that came with my hand.

The fact that Werner and I were wildly in love and would have married anyway, fat purse or no, made the match all the better.

He saw my gaze and his glance at me, as intoxicating as the wine we were drinking and just as golden, made my heart skip a beat. How had I managed to find this man, my heart, my soul mate, out of all the men in this world? He stood a scant few inches taller than me, which made me happy. As a taller woman, I worried that I would be fettered to a man who scarcely reached my chin. Instead, I had landed this black-haired prince. Even amid the chaos of these people, my attention focused on one man and one man only.

My mother kept raising her embellished goblet to us, as did the king. My father was too busy eating the rich breads that accompanied our pheasant dinner, his short arms struggling to reach around his portly belly. But even my father's desire to eat rather than celebrate couldn't dampen my spirits. I just needed my mother to set her goblet back on the table already, so I might sneak out the back and hide in the garden shadows with this man who'd been crafted from my dreams.

I didn't tell anyone but my grandmother that I had tried out a love spell on him. My heart was on fire for Werner since I'd first met him. We had attended a Christmas ball at the Seta Castle the year before, and I knew the image I presented — my bold red gown fitted tightly to my body, red and white ribbons encrusted with crystals woven into my hair. Oh, my image in my small bedroom mirror told me what a vision I was!

That night, Werner had seen me, cut through the crowd of eager subjects, and came straight for me. He'd pursued me and me alone. My heart had fluttered as erratically as a newly-birthed butterfly when he grasped my hand in his large, warm one and asked for the next dance. For the rest of the night, he never left my side.

When I poured my girlish desires on my grandmother's patient ear, she had smiled, crinkling her already wrinkled blue eyes, and reached into her cupboard for several leather satchels and a pestle. I had sat mesmerized as her thin, bowed body worked earnestly, mixing the herbs and petals into a bowl, ground it with the pestle, then reached a gnarled hand to me.

"Hold still," she'd commanded in her surprisingly strong voice and plucked a single hair from my head.

"Ow!" I'd yelped as she smiled and added my hair to the bowl, grinding it in with the rest. Then she had poured the mixture into a fresh satchel.

"The next time you see your man, pour this in his drink. 'Twill make him fall in love with you."

At the time, I didn't take the proffered satchel, not at first. "Grandmother, he's a prince! What would he do with the likes of me? 'Tis not like we might wed or anything."

She had waggled her finger at me and pushed the satchel into my hand. "In that you are wrong. Most magic is little more than putting your desires out into the universe. These trappings, they help make it real. You are the stunningly beautiful daughter of a wealthy baron. The prince could do no better than to wed you."

I had dropped my gaze, smiling with pride at my grandmother's boasts. She was my grandmother, so she had to say it, but her words were the sweetest music to my ears. I had always been the apple of her eye, the child she'd wished my mother to be, and that made me love her all the more.

In the end, I had grasped the satchel and tucked it into my fitted bodice. Then I added it to his wine the next time he and his father visited our manse.

Then Werner kissed me for the first time under the stars later that night. His lips tasted of the sweet wine and were softer than my velvet gown. The stars winked at me as the light touch of his lips caressed mine, as though the universe approved of my choice.

Did the love potion help? Maybe.

I wasn't about to doubt the magic my grandmother knew. Her magic always seemed to work.

Start Before the Magic Mirror today!

Fairy Tale Notes

I love fairy tales. Not just the primary princess story (though Cinderella is one of my favorites), but back stories. I adore back stories of the different characters. We see them in this one moment in time, but what led to that? What happened to those characters to now make them behave as they do? What from their past is motivating them now?

Those are the stories I love to read. It's like a sneak peek into a different world, one outside the story, delving into the characters in such a way as to make them richer, to make us care about them more.

For me, the villains in our favorite fairy tales have intrigued me. What trauma or event shook them to their core so hard that they are now a villain? Because, as we know, villains don't start out that way. The best villains were ordinary people until something happened.

So what happened? That's what I love to read.

A few films and television shows have come out in the past several years, providing a back story to some of our favorite villains, or show us, perhaps, they aren't as villainous as we believed them to be – that they are acting with the best knowledge they have or to help a situation that we didn't know about.

Those are the best fairy tale backstory surprises.

These stories are a move away from my usual historical romances. They are not as entrenched in history; they are a bit darker; and the don't necessarily end in the traditional Happily Ever After (gasp!). In this series, I tried to imagine, what would it be like for those villains before they were painted as a villain. Are they really as evil as they are shown in the princess story? What if I were in their shoes – what would I have done? Would the outcome have been any different? Could I have been painted as the villain then?

Oh, what might have happened! This series delves into those complex ideas, that maybe our villains aren't the villain we believe them to be.

I hope you enjoy these backstories as much as I do.

A Thank You to My Readers –

Thank you to my loyal readers – for you I am eternally grateful. Thank you for trying something a bit different from me.

A huge thank you to the great fairy tale stories I've been reading as of late. I love the myriad of those variations!

As always, I need to thank my kids and family for always supporting me. Even though writing takes me away from them, they are my best cheerleaders. I couldn't do this without their support.

I also need to thank my Facebook groups and writing colleagues who provide guidance and advice when needed. We are a tight-knit group, and you all are so wonderful for helping me along this path.

Finally, and just as eternally, I need to thank Michael, the man in my life who has been so supportive of my career shift to focus more on writing, and who makes a great sounding board for ideas. Thank you, babe, for putting up with this and for keeping me from being a villain and for giving me my own Happily Ever After.

About the Author

Michelle Deerwester-Dalrymple is a professor of writing and an author. She started reading when she was 3 years old, writing when she was 4, and published her first poem at age 16. She has written articles and essays on a variety of topics, including several texts on writing for middle and high school students. She has written fifteen books under a variety of pen names and is also slowly working on a novel inspired by actual events. She lives in California with her family of seven.

Find Michelle on your favorite social media sites and sign up for her newsletter here:

https://linktr.ee/mddalrympleauthor

Also by the Author:

As Michelle Deerwester-Dalrymple

Glen Highland Romance

The Courtship of the Glen –Prequel Short Novella
To Dance in the Glen – Book 1
The Lady of the Glen – Book 2
The Exile of the Glen – Book 3
The Jewel of the Glen – Book 4
The Seduction of the Glen – Book 5
The Warrior of the Glen – Book 6
An Echo in the Glen – Book 7
The Blackguard of the Glen – Book 8
The Christmas in the Glen – coming soon

The Celtic Highland Maidens

The Maiden of the Storm
The Maiden of the Grove
The Maiden of the Celts
The Roman of the North
The Maiden of the Stones
The Maiden of the Wood
The Maiden of the Loch – coming soon

The *Before* Series

Before the Glass Slipper
Before the Magic Mirror

Before the Cursed Beast
Before the Mermaid's Tale

<u>Glen Coe Highlanders</u>
Highland Burn – Book 1
Highland Breath – Book 2

<u>Historical Fevered Series</u>
The Highlander's Scarred Heart
The Highlander's Legacy
The Highlander's Return
Her Knight's Second Chance
The Highlander's Vow
Her Knight's Christmas Gift
The Outlaw Trilogy:
Her Outlaw Highlander – book 1
Outlaw Highlander Found—book 2
Outlaw Highlander Home – book 3

<u>As M.D. Dalrymple - Men in Uniform</u>
Night Shift – Book 1
Day Shift – Book 2
Overtime – Book 3
Holiday Pay – Book 4
School Resource Officer – book 5
Undercover – book 6
Holdover – book 7